# POEMS FOR CHRISTMAS

# POEMS FOR CHRISTMAS

With an introduction by
JUDITH FLANDERS

Edited by
GABY MORGAN

MACMILLAN COLLECTOR'S LIBRARY

This collection first published 2019 by Macmillan Collector's Library

This edition first published 2024 by Macmillan Collector's Library
an imprint of Pan Macmillan
The Smithson, 6 Briset Street, London ECIM 5NR
*EU representative:* Macmillan Publishers Ireland Ltd, 1st Floor,
The Liffey Trust Centre, 117–126 Sheriff Street Upper,
Dublin 1, DOI YC43
Associated companies throughout the world
www.panmacmillan.com

ISBN 978-1-0350-4911-0

Selection and arrangement copyright © Gaby Morgan 2019
Introduction copyright © Judith Flanders 2019

1 3 5 7 9 8 6 4 2

A CIP catalogue record for this book is available from the British Library.

Cover and endpaper design: Daisy Bates, Pan Macmillan Art Department
Typeset by Jouve (UK), Milton Keynes
Printed and bound in China by Imago

Visit **www.panmacmillan.com** to read more about all our books
and to buy them. You will also find features, author interviews and
news of any author events, and you can sign up for e-newsletters
so that you're always first to hear about our new releases.

# Contents

*Introduction* xiii

## CHRISTMAS IS COMING

Christmas is Coming *Traditional* 3

A Christmas Blessing *Traditional* 4

Now Thrice Welcome, Christmas *Traditional* 5

Deck the Halls *Traditional* 6

We Wish You a Merry Christmas *Traditional* 7

Pudding Charms *Charlotte Druitt Cole* 8

The Christmas Pudding *Traditional* 9

Christmas Plum Pudding *Clifton Bingham* 10

A Dish for a Poet *Traditional* 11

Yule Log *Robert Herrick* 13

Minstrels *William Wordsworth* 14

Old Christmastide *Sir Walter Scott* 15

December *John Clare* 18

French Noel *William Morris* 23

Wassail, Wassail *Traditional* 26

Here We Come A-Wassailing *Traditional* 28

Nowell Sing We *Traditional* 30

# Contents

## I SING OF A MAIDEN

I Sing of a Maiden *Traditional* 33

A Virgin Most Pure *Traditional* 34

The Mother of God *W. B. Yeats* 36

The Cherry Tree Carol *Traditional* 37

Joseph *G. K. Chesterton* 40

The Angel Gabriel *Traditional*
*tr. Sabine Baring-Gould* 41

Once in Royal David's City
*Cecil Frances Alexander* 42

O Little Town of Bethlehem *Phillips Brooks* 44

Away in a Manger *Traditional* 46

The Old Hark *Traditional* 47

Angels, from the Realms of Glory
*James Montgomery* 49

Hark! The Herald Angels Sing *Charles Wesley* 50

A Hymn for Christmas Day *Traditional* 52

Joy to the World! *Isaac Watts* 54

In Dulci Jubilo *Traditional* 55

Christmas – A Song of Joy at Dawn
*Traditional* 56

O Come, All Ye Faithful *Traditional*
*tr. F. Oakeley and W. T. Brooke* 58

*Contents*

# PEACE AND LULLABIES

Peace *Henry Vaughan* 63

A Child this Day is Born *Traditional* 64

Silent Night *Joseph Mohr tr. John Freeman Young* 66

Christus Natus Est *Countee Cullen* 67

On Christmas Day to My Heart *Clement Paman* 69

An Ode of the Birth of Our Saviour
*Robert Herrick* 71

The House of Christmas *G. K. Chesterton* 73

The Nativity of Our Lord and Saviour
Jesus Christ *Christopher Smart* 75

New Prince, New Pomp *Robert Southwell* 77

Past Three O'Clock *George Ratcliffe Woodward* 79

Love Came Down at Christmas *Christina Rossetti* 81

Before the Paling of the Stars *Christina Rossetti* 82

The Coventry Carol *Traditional* 83

A Christmas Carol *G. K. Chesterton* 84

A Cradle Song *William Blake* 85

The Rocking Carol *Percy Dearmer* 87

Infant Holy *Traditional tr. Edith M.G. Reed* 88

Sing Lullaby *Sabine Baring-Gould* 89

Welcome to Heaven's King *Traditional* 91

Hymn for Christmas Day *John Byrom* 92

It Was on Christmas Day *Traditional* 94

I Saw a Stable *Mary Elizabeth Coleridge* 95

# Contents

## HOLLY AND IVY

Holly *Christina Rossetti* 99

Advent *Christina Rossetti* 100

Green Grow'th the Holly *Traditional* 101

Lo, How a Rose E'er Blooming *Traditional
tr. Theodore Baker and Harriet R. K. Spaeth* 102

The Mahogany Tree *William Makepeace
Thackeray* 103

The Holly and the Ivy *Traditional* 105

The First Tree in the Greenwood *Traditional* 107

## BIRDS AND BEASTS

Eddi's Service *Rudyard Kipling* 111

The Oxen *Thomas Hardy* 113

Sheep in Winter *John Clare* 114

While Shepherds Watched Their Flocks
*Nahum Tate* 115

Go, Tell it on the Mountain *Traditional* 116

The Shepherds' Carol *Traditional* 117

Out in the Dark *Edward Thomas* 118

Birds at Winter Nightfall *Thomas Hardy* 119

Little Robin Redbreast *Traditional* 120

*Contents*

## SNOW AND ICE

Christmas Night *Traditional* 123

The First Nowell *Traditional* 124

Snow Storm *John Clare* 126

See, Amid the Winter's Snow *Edward Caswall* 127

A Winter Night *William Barnes* 129

Winter *Gerard Manley Hopkins* 130

Winter-Time *Robert Louis Stevenson* 132

Snow *Edward Thomas* 133

*from* As You Like It *William Shakespeare* 134

Up in the Morning Early *Robert Burns* 135

In Tenebris *Ford Madox Ford* 136

In the Bleak Midwinter *Christina Rossetti* 137

It Came Upon the Midnight Clear
*Edmund Hamilton Sears* 139

Snow in the Suburbs *Thomas Hardy* 141

*from* The Prelude *William Wordsworth* 142

*from* Frost at Midnight *Samuel Taylor Coleridge* 144

A Frosty Day *Lord de Tabley* 145

Ice on the Highway *Thomas Hardy* 146

Now Winter Nights Enlarge *Thomas Campion* 147

# Contents

## NATIVITY

Christmas *George Herbert* 151

The Nativity *Henry Vaughan* 153

Nativity *John Donne* 155

Upon Christ His Birth *Sir John Suckling* 156

Noel: Christmas Eve, 1913 *Robert Bridges* 157

*from* In Memoriam *Alfred, Lord Tennyson* 159

Christmas Eve *Christina Rossetti* 161

## THE EARTHLY PARADISE

*from* The Earthly Paradise *William Morris* 165

God Rest You Merry, Gentlemen *Traditional* 167

Carol *Ben Jonson* 169

Christmas at Sea *Robert Louis Stevenson* 170

Christmas in India *Rudyard Kipling* 173

From East to West, From Shore to Shore
*Traditional* 175

## KINGS

The Three Kings *Henry Wadsworth Longfellow* 179

We Three Kings *John Henry Hopkins* 182

As With Gladness Men of Old *William
Chatterton Dix* 184

Good King Wenceslas *John Mason Neale* 186

## Contents

The Mystic Magi *Robert Stephen Hawker* 188

Kings Came Riding *Charles Williams* 189


### I SAW THREE SHIPS

I Saw Three Ships Come Sailing In *Traditional* 193

As I Sat on a Sunny Bank *Traditional* 195

To-morrow Shall Be My Dancing Day
*Traditional* 196

The True Christmas *Henry Vaughan* 197

A Visit from St Nicholas *Clement Clarke Moore* 198

What Billy Wanted *Traditional* 200

A Little Christmas Card *Traditional* 201

The Twelve Days of Christmas *Traditional* 202


### NEW YEAR

Another Christmas Gone *Traditional* 207

The Old Year *John Clare* 208

The New Year *Traditional* 209

New Year *Christopher Smart* 210

The New Year *Traditional* 212

Auld Lang Syne *Robert Burns* 213

Ring Out, Wild Bells *Alfred, Lord Tennyson* 214

Farewell Old Year *Traditional* 216

New Every Morning *Susan Coolidge* 217

# Contents

The Year  *Ella Wheeler Wilcox*  218

*from* The Tempest  *William Shakespeare*  219


Index of Poets  221

Index of Titles  225

Index of First Lines  231

## Introduction

JUDITH FLANDERS

In the sixteenth century, the poet Thomas Tusser advised his readers: 'At Christmas play and make good cheere / For Christmas comes but once a yeere.' And while that has not changed over the centuries – not the play, nor the good cheer, nor the indubitable fact that the holiday does, indeed, only come around once a year – almost everything else we know about Christmas has altered beyond recognition since his day.

Or has it? Today Christmas is a medley, a holiday of family and friends, of food and drink, of gifts and leisure, even as the seasonal grumps tell us that the 'true' meaning of Christmas has been lost, that in the Good Old Days – days that shift from the nineteenth century, to the 1950s, to whenever the speaker was a child – in those Good Old Days, Things Were Better: more religious, more sacrosanct, more, well, basically, more serious.

But were they? It only took a few decades after the first Christmas was celebrated in the Roman Empire for an archbishop to have to warn his flock against too much seasonal dancing and 'feasting to excess', with too little respect paid to the religious meaning of the day. For early Christmases, every bit as much as today, revolved around eating and drinking, with religion playing a minor chord in the background. It was instead a holiday of holly and ivy, festive trees, consumption, mumming, dressing up, singing and, just as the archbishop worried, dancing.

*Introduction*

By the sixteenth century, the greatest in the land were holding lavish banquets interspersed with masques, plays with songs and dances; civic authorities and guilds staged great street parades to entertain the masses and promote their own grandeur; while the prosperous entertained their nearest and dearest with food and drink. And the working people went house to house 'wassailing', or toasting, the residents in exchange for food, beer and sometimes cash, as was recorded in traditional wassailing songs.

The first wassailing song in this anthology, 'Wassail, Wassail', represents a different, agricultural wassailing tradition, where the singers drank a toast to the farm's animals to ensure a good agricultural year, or wassailed the crops themselves to encourage a good harvest.

Because Christmas songs were, for the most part, not religious. Of course the church had its own music for the time of year, but the songs of the people, by the people, were about things they enjoyed – about dancing, singing, drinking and eating. A 'carol' was not even originally a song sung in December – it was first used to describe a secular French spring song accompanied by a dance. (That carols were not originally for Christmas can be seen by our continuing to say 'Christmas carol' instead of just 'carol', even though today we sing carols at no other time of the year.)

Defining a carol itself ranges from the difficult to the impossible. The *Oxford English Dictionary* says a carol is 'A song or hymn of joy sung at Christmas in celebration of the Nativity'. This, however, overlooks the hundreds of carols in praise of trees, holly, ivy, drinking and feasting, including many favourites included in this book, such as 'Deck the Halls', which was a Welsh carol written probably in the sixteenth century; or carols that

*xiv*

are really folk songs or ballads, such as 'The Cherry Tree Carol'; or African-American spirituals like 'Go, Tell it on the Mountain'. The simplest definition, perhaps, is that a carol is anything people decide is one.

Because carols are mostly songs of the people, by the people and for the people. They were disregarded by the great and good, and therefore, to a large degree, were unrecorded for posterity. It was only in the nineteenth century, when a new love of 'olde' England and its traditions emerged, that the songs of the people, including their seasonal Christmas songs, began to be collected in printed form, in expensive books for middle-class readers. But as they were revived and gained a new audience, some carols may have been not actually revived, but invented, with a new and artificial history created for them.

And that's true of so much to do with Christmas. We half-know things, and other things are made up, and we imagine others, and somehow, they all merge together to become the 'true' Christmas. Because fabricating history, and sweet stories, is one of our most popular Christmas traditions. The story of 'Silent Night' is a perfect example of the genre. In 1820, goes the delightful and entirely fictitious story, the church organ in the small town of Oberndorf, in what is now Austria, fell into disrepair just before the all-important Christmas services, and so the curate (Joseph Mohr, words) and the assistant organist (Franz Xaver Gruber, music) hastily cobbled together a carol to a guitar accompaniment. In reality, while Mohr and Gruber were indeed the carol's creators, history shows that the church's organ continued to give good service for years afterwards. More prosaically, the piece was heard by a visiting folk-music enthusiast who included it in a professional concert in Leipzig in 1823 as a Tyrolean folk song, despite it not being a folk song and Oberndorf not being located in the Tyrol.

Some of our most treasured traditions follow this same imaginary, mythical development. Carols were, as we have seen, songs of the people until well into the nineteenth century. They had little recognition among the middle classes, and were certainly never sung in churches. But by 1880, a new tradition was emerging. The then Bishop of Truro, later to become Archbishop of Canterbury, had his finger on the pulse, and that year he planned a Christmas Eve concert complete with carols and readings. It was so popular that other churches rapidly followed, either taking over his programme wholesale, or creating their own. By 1918, King's College, Cambridge began its celebrated Christmas Eve Festival of Nine Lessons and Carols, based on the Bishop of Truro's evening.

King's College's own website carefully gives this 1918 date; the BBC, however, which broadcasts the concert religiously (in both senses of the word), has historically been more – shall we say – elastic with the truth. By 1931 the BBC's publicity material promoted this thirteen-year-old concert as a tradition of the ages; by 1939 it had aged exponentially: 'The festival has been held since the chapel was built nearly 500 years ago,' it intoned. For perhaps the single rule of Christmas to hold true is: if something is referred to as 'traditional', it is new; if it is called 'ancient', it is recent; and if it is both – well, if it is both, it is dearly loved, and you pit boring things like facts against strong emotions at your peril.

A seventeenth-century booklet, 'Make Room for Christmas', drew its own picture of the very best

*Introduction*

Christmas, portraying it as a holiday made up of neigh-
bourly visits, of apples roasting by a welcoming fire, of
'melodious Carrols', concluding, with a flourish, 'and so
we'l be higly pigly one with another'. And in truth,
Christmas is all higgledy-piggledy, as our customs and
traditions, songs and stories, family and friends pile up
in our imaginations in a glorious jumble of Christmases
past, Christmases fictional, Christmases on television
and radio, the Christmases we have had, the Christ-
mases we believe others have, and the Christmases we
hope to have.

Christmas comes but once a year, but the holiday,
and all it represents, is rooted deep in our imaginations.
These Christmas poems, whether old, new or a magic
Christmas hybrid, are mysteriously both youthfully
invigorating and contain the wisdom of the ancients, as
each Christmas season renews itself. And in so doing,
the poems, and Christmas itself, allow us, too, to renew
ourselves.

# POEMS FOR CHRISTMAS

# CHRISTMAS IS COMING

# Christmas is Coming

Christmas is coming,
  The geese are getting fat,
Please to put a penny
  In the old man's hat.
If you haven't got a penny,
  A ha'penny will do;
If you haven't got a ha'penny,
  Then God bless you!

*Traditional*

# A Christmas Blessing

God bless the master of this house,
   The mistress also,
And all the little children
   That round the table go;
And all your kin and kinsfolk
   That dwell both far and near:
I wish you a Merry Christmas
   And a Happy New Year.

*Traditional*

# Now Thrice Welcome, Christmas

Now thrice welcome, Christmas,
  Which brings us good cheer,
Minced pies and plum porridge,
  Good ale and strong beer;
With pig, goose and capon,
  The best that may be,
So well doth the weather
  And our stomachs agree.

*Traditional*

# Deck the Halls

Deck the halls with boughs of holly,
'Tis the season to be jolly,
Don we now our gay apparel,
Troll the ancient Yuletide carol.

See the blazing Yule before us.
Strike the harp and join the chorus,
Follow me in merry measure,
While I tell of Yuletide treasure.

Fast away the old year passes,
Hail the new, ye lads and lasses,
Sing we joyous all together,
Heedless of the wind and weather.

*Traditional*

# We Wish You a Merry Christmas

We wish you a merry Christmas,
We wish you a merry Christmas,
We wish you a merry Christmas,
And a happy New Year.

*Good tidings we bring*
*To you and your kin,*
*We wish you a merry Christmas,*
*And a happy New Year.*

Now bring us some figgy pudding,
Now bring us some figgy pudding,
Now bring us some figgy pudding,
And bring some out here.
  *Chorus*

For we all like figgy pudding,
For we all like figgy pudding,
For we all like figgy pudding,
So bring some out here.
  *Chorus*

And we won't go until we've had some,
And we won't go until we've had some,
And we won't go until we've had some,
So bring some out here.
  *Chorus*

*Traditional*

# Pudding Charms

Our Christmas pudding was made in November,
All they put in it, I quite well remember:
Currants and raisins, and sugar and spice,
Orange peel, lemon peel – everything nice
Mixed up together, and put in a pan.
'When you've stirred it,' said Mother, 'as much
    as you can,
We'll cover it over, that nothing may spoil it,
And then, in the copper, tomorrow we'll boil it.'
That night, when we children were all fast asleep,
A real fairy godmother came crip-a-creep!
She wore a red cloak, and a tall steeple hat
(Though nobody saw her but Tinker, the cat!)
And out of her pocket a thimble she drew,
A button of silver, a silver horse-shoe,
And, whisp'ring a charm in the pudding pan
    popped them,
Then flew up the chimney directly she dropped
    them;
And even old Tinker pretended he slept
(With Tinker a secret is sure to be kept!),
So nobody knew, until Christmas came round,
And there, in the pudding, these treasures were
    found.

*Charlotte Druitt Cole*

# The Christmas Pudding

Into the basin
put the plums,
stir-about, stir-about,
stir-about.

Next the good
white flour comes,
stir-about, stir-about,
stir-about.

Sugar and peel
and eggs and spice,
stir-about, stir-about,
stir-about.

Mix them and fix them
and cook them twice,
stir-about, stir-about,
stir-about.

*Traditional*

# Christmas Plum Pudding

When they sat down that day to dine
The beef was good, the turkey fine
But oh, the pudding!

The goose was tender and so nice,
That everybody had some twice –
But oh, that pudding!

It's coming, that they knew quite well,
They didn't see, they couldn't smell,
That fine plum pudding!

It came, an object of delight!
Their mouths watered at the sight
Of that plum pudding!

When they had finished, it was true,
They'd also put a finish to
That poor plum pudding!

*Clifton Bingham (1859–1913)*

# A Dish for a Poet

Take a large olive, stone it and then stuff it with a
  paste made of anchovy, capers, and oil.
Put the olive inside a trussed and boned bec-figue.
Put the bec-figue inside a fat ortolan.
Put the ortolan inside a boned lark.
Put the stuffed lark inside a boned thrush.
Put the thrush inside a fat quail.
Put the quail, wrapped in vine-leaves, inside a
  boned lapwing.
Put the lapwing inside a boned golden plover.
Put the plover inside a fat, boned, red-legged
  partridge.
Put the partridge inside a young, boned, and well-
  hung woodcock.
Put the woodcock, rolled in bread-crumbs, inside a
  boned teal.
Put the teal inside a boned guinea-fowl.
Put the guinea-fowl, well larded, inside a young and
  boned tame duck.
Put the duck inside a boned and fat fowl.
Put the fowl inside a well-hung pheasant.
Put the pheasant inside a boned and fat wild goose.
Put the goose inside a fine turkey.
Put the turkey inside a boned bustard.
Having arranged your roast after this fashion, place it
  in a large saucepan with onions stuffed with cloves,
  carrots, small squares of ham, celery, mignonette,
  several strips of bacon well-seasoned, pepper, salt,
  spice, coriander seeds, and two cloves of garlic.
Seal the saucepan hermetically by closing it with
  pastry. Then put it for ten hours over a gentle fire,

and arrange it so that the heat can penetrate evenly. An oven moderately heated will suit better than the hearth.

Before serving, remove the pastry, put the roast on a hot dish after having removed the grease – if there is any – and serve.

*Traditional*

# Yule Log

Come, bring with a noise,
　My merrie, merrie boyes,
The Christmas Log to the firing;
　While my good Dame, she
　Bids ye all be free;
And drink to your hearts' desiring.

With the last yeeres brand
　Light the new block, and
For good successe in his spending,
　On your Psaltries play,
　That sweet luck may
Come while the log is a-teending.

Drink now the strong Beere,
　Cut the white loafe here,
The while the meat is a-shredding;
　For the rare Mince-Pie
　And the Plums stand by
To fill the paste that's a-kneading.

*Robert Herrick (1591–1674)*

# Minstrels

The minstrels played their Christmas tune
Tonight beneath my cottage-eaves;
While, smitten by a lofty moon,
The encircling laurels, thick with leaves,
Gave back a rich and dazzling sheen,
That overpowered their natural green.

Through hill and valley every breeze
Had sunk to rest with folded wings:
Keen was the air, but could not freeze,
Nor check, the music of the strings;
So stout and hardy were the band
That scraped the chords with strenuous hand.

And who but listened? – till was paid
Respect to every inmate's claim,
The greeting given, the music played
In honour of each household name,
Duly pronounced with lusty call,
And 'Merry Christmas' wished to all.

*William Wordsworth (1770–1850)*

# Old Christmastide

Heap on more wood! – the wind is chill;
But let it whistle as it will,
We'll keep our Christmas merry still.
Each age has deemed the new-born year
The fittest time for festal cheer.
Even heathen yet, the savage Dane
At Iol more deep the mead did drain;
High on the beach his galley drew,
And feasted all his pirate crew;
Then in his low and pine-built hall,
Where shields and axes decked the wall,
They gorged upon the half-dressed steer;
Caroused in seas of sable beer;
While round, in brutal jest, were thrown
The half-gnawed rib and marrow-bone,
Or listened all, in grim delight,
While scalds yelled out the joy of fight,
Then forth in frenzy would they hie,
While wildly loose their red locks fly;
And, dancing round the blazing pile,
They make such barbarous mirth the while,
As best might to the mind recall
The boisterous joys of Odin's hall.
And well our Christian sire of old
Loved when the year its course had rolled,
And brought blithe Christmas back again,
With all his hospitable train.
Domestic and religious rite
Gave honour to the holy night:
On Christmas eve the bells were rung;
On Christmas eve the mass was sung;

That only night, in all the year,
Saw the stoled priest the chalice rear.
The damsel donned her kirtle sheen;
The hall was dressed with holly green;
Forth to the wood did merry men go,
To gather in the mistletoe;
Then opened wide the baron's hall
To vassal, tenant, serf, and all;
Power laid his rod of rule aside,
And ceremony doffed his pride.
The heir, with roses in his shoes,
That night might village partner choose;
The lord, underogating, share
The vulgar game of 'post and pair.'
All hailed, with uncontrolled delight,
And general voice, the happy night
That to the cottage, as the crown,
Brought tidings of salvation down.
The fire, with well-dried logs supplied,
Went roaring up the chimney wide;
The huge hall-table's oaken face,
Scrubbed till it shone, the day to grace,
Bore then upon its massive board
No mark to part the squire and lord.
Then was brought in the lusty brawn
By old blue-coated serving man;
Then the grim boar's head frowned on high,
Crested with bays and rosemary.
Well can the green-garbed ranger tell,
How, when, and where the monster fell;
What dogs before his death he tore,
And all the baiting of the boar.
The Wassail round, in good brown bowls,
Garnished with ribbons, blithely trowls.

There the huge sirloin reeked; hard by
Plum-porridge stood, and Christmas pie;
Nor failed old Scotland to produce,
At such high tide, her savoury goose.
Then came the merry masquers in,
And carols roared with blithesome din;
If unmelodious was the song,
It was a hearty note, and strong,
Who lists may in their mumming see
Traces of ancient mystery;
White shirts supplied the masquerade,
And smutted cheeks the vizors made:
But, what masquers, richly dight,
Can boast of bosoms half so light?
England was merry England, when
Old Christmas brought his sports again.
'Twas Christmas broached the mightiest ale;
'Twas Christmas told the merriest tale;
A Christmas gambol oft could cheer
The poor man's heart through half the year.

*Sir Walter Scott (1771–1832)*

# December

Glad Christmas comes, and every hearth
  Makes room to give him welcome now,
E'en want will dry its tears in mirth,
  And crown him with a holly bough;
Though tramping 'neath a winter sky,
  O'er snowy paths and rimy stiles,
The housewife sets her spinning by
  To bid him welcome with her smiles.

Each house is swept the day before,
  And windows stuck with ever-greens,
The snow is besom'd from the door,
  And comfort crowns the cottage scenes.
Gilt holly, with its thorny pricks,
  And yew and box, with berries small,
These deck the unused candlesticks,
  And pictures hanging by the wall.

Neighbours resume their annual cheer,
  Wishing, with smiles and spirits high,
Glad Christmas and a happy year,
  To every morning passer-by;
Milkmaids their Christmas journeys go,
  Accompanied with favour'd swain;
And children pace the crumping snow,
  To taste their granny's cake again.

The shepherd, now no more afraid,
  Since custom doth the chance bestow,
Starts up to kiss the giggling maid
  Beneath the branch of mistletoe

That 'neath each cottage beam is seen,
    With pearl-like berries shining gay;
The shadow still of what hath been,
    Which fashion yearly fades away.

The singing wates, a merry throng,
    At early morn, with simple skill,
Yet imitate the angels song,
    And chant their Christmas ditty still;
And, 'mid the storm that dies and swells
    By fits – in hummings softly steals
The music of the village bells,
    Ringing round their merry peals.

When this is past, a merry crew,
    Bedeck'd in masks and ribbons gay,
The 'Morris-dance,' their sports renew,
    And act their winter evening play.
The clown turn'd king, for penny-praise,
    Storms with the actor's strut and swell;
And Harlequin, a laugh to raise,
    Wears his hunch-back and tinkling bell.

And oft for pence and spicy ale,
    With winter nosegays pinn'd before,
The wassail-singer tells her tale,
    And drawls her Christmas carols o'er.
While 'prentice boy, with ruddy face,
    And rime-bepowder'd, dancing locks,
From door to door with happy pace,
    Runs round to claim his 'Christmas box.'

The block upon the fire is put,
    To sanction custom's old desires;

And many a fagot's bands are cut,
  For the old farmers' Christmas fires;
Where loud-tongued Gladness joins the throng,
  And Winter meets the warmth of May,
Till feeling soon the heat too strong,
  He rubs his shins, and draws away.

While snows the window-panes bedim,
  The fire curls up a sunny charm,
Where, creaming o'er the pitcher's rim,
  The flowering ale is set to warm;
Mirth, full of joy as summer bees,
  Sits there, its pleasures to impart,
And children, 'tween their parent's knees,
  Sing scraps of carols o'er by heart.

And some, to view the winter weathers,
  Climb up the window-seat with glee,
Likening the snow to falling feathers,
  In Fancy's infant ecstasy;
Laughing, with superstitious love,
  O'er visions wild that youth supplies,
Of people pulling geese above,
  And keeping Christmas in the skies.

As tho' the homestead trees were drest,
  In lieu of snow, with dancing leaves;
As tho' the sun-dried martin's nest,
  Instead of i'cles hung the eaves;
The children hail the happy day –
  As if the snow were April's grass,
And pleas'd, as 'neath the warmth of May,
  Sport o'er the water froze to glass.

Thou day of happy sound and mirth,
    That long with childish memory stays,
How blest around the cottage hearth
    I met thee in my younger days!
Harping, with rapture's dreaming joys,
    On presents which thy coming found,
The welcome sight of little toys,
    The Christmas gift of cousins round.

The wooden horse with arching head,
    Drawn upon wheels around the room;
The gilded coach of gingerbread,
    And many-colour'd sugar plum;
Gilt cover'd books for pictures sought,
    Or stories childhood loves to tell,
With many an urgent promise bought,
    To get to-morrow's lesson well.

And many a thing, a minute's sport,
    Left broken on the sanded floor,
When we would leave our play, and court
    Our parents' promises for more.
Tho' manhood bids such raptures die,
    And throws such toys aside as vain,
Yet memory loves to turn her eye,
    And count past pleasures o'er again.

Around the glowing hearth at night,
    The harmless laugh and winter tale
Go round, while parting friends delight
    To toast each other o'er their ale;
The cotter oft with quiet zeal
    Will musing o'er his Bible lean;

While in the dark the lovers steal
  To kiss and toy behind the screen.

Old customs! Oh! I love the sound,
  However simple they may be:
Whate'er with time hath sanction found,
  Is welcome, and is dear to me.
Pride grows above simplicity,
  And spurns them from her haughty mind,
And soon the poet's song will be
  The only refuge they can find.

*John Clare (1793–1864)*

# French Noel

Masters, in this Hall,
  Hear ye news to-day
Brought from over sea,
  And ever I you pray.

*Nowell! Nowell! Nowell! Nowell sing we clear*
*Holpen are all folk on earth, Born is God's Son so dear:*
*Nowell! Nowell! Nowell! Nowell sing we loud!*
*God to-day hath poor folk rais'd, And cast down the proud.*

Going over the hills,
  Through the milk-white snow,
Heard I ewes bleat
  While the wind did blow.

Shepherds many an one
  Sat among the sheep,
No man spake more word
  Than they had been asleep.

Quoth I 'Fellows mine,
  Why this guise sit ye?
Making but dull cheer,
  Shepherds though ye be?

'Shepherds should of right
  Leap and dance and sing;
Thus to see ye sit
  Is a right strange thing.'

Quoth these fellows then,
  'To Bethlem town we go,
To see a mighty Lord
  Lie in a manger low.'

'How name ye this Lord,
  Shepherds?' then said I.
'Very *God*,' they said,
  'Come from Heaven high.'

Then to Bethlem town
  We went two and two
And in a sorry place
  Heard the oxen low.

Therein did we see
  A sweet and goodly May
And a fair old man;
  Upon the straw She lay.

And a little Child
  On Her arm had She;
'Wot ye Who this is?'
  Said the hinds to me.

Ox and ass Him know,
  Kneeling on their knee:
Wondrous joy had I
  This little Babe to see.

This is Christ the Lord
　　Masters, be ye glad!
Christmas is come in,
　　And no folk should be sad.

*Nowell! Nowell! Nowell! Nowell sing we clear*
*Holpen are all folk on earth, Born is God's Son so dear:*
*Nowell! Nowell! Nowell! Nowell sing we loud!*
*God to-day hath poor folk rais'd, And cast down the proud.*

　　　　　　　　　　　*William Morris (1834–1896)*

# Wassail, Wassail

Wassail, Wassail, all over the town!
Our toast it is white, and our ale it is brown,
Our bowl it is made of the white maple tree;
With the wassailing bowl we'll drink to thee.

So here is to Cherry and to his right cheek,
Pray God send our master a good piece of beef,
And a good piece of beef that may we all see;
With the wassailing bowl we'll drink to thee.

And here is to Dobbin and to his right eye,
Pray God send our master a good Christmas pie,
And a good Christmas pie that may we all see;
With our wassailing bowl we'll drink to thee.

So here is to Broad May and to her broad horn,
May God send our master a good crop of corn,
And a good crop of corn that may we all see;
With the wassailing bowl we'll drink to thee.

And here is to Fillpail and to her left ear,
Pray God send our master a happy New Year,
And a happy New Year as e'er he did see;
With our wassailing bowl we'll drink to thee.

And here is to Colly and to her long tail,
Pray God send our master he never may fail
A bowl of strong beer; I pray you draw near,
And our jolly wassail it's then you shall hear.

Come, butler, come fill us a bowl of the best,
Then we hope that your soul in heaven may rest;
But if you do draw us a bowl of the small,
Then down shall go butler, bowl and all.

Then here's to the maid in the lily white smock,
Who tripped to the door and slipped back the lock!
Who tripped to the door and pulled back the pin,
For to let these jolly wassailers in.

*Traditional*

# Here We Come A-Wassailing

Here we come a-wassailing
Among the leaves so green;
Here we come a-wandering
So fair to be seen.

*Love and joy come to you,*
*And to you your wassail too,*
*And God bless you, and send you a*
*    happy new year,*
*And God send you a happy new year.*

Our wassail cup is made
Of the rosemary tree,
And so is your beer
Of the best barley.

We are not daily beggars
That beg from door to door,
But we are neighbours' children
Whom you have seen before.

Call up the butler of this house
Put on his golden ring;
Let him bring us up a glass of beer,
And better shall we sing.

We have got a little purse
Of stretching leather skin;
We want a little of your money
To line it well within.

Bring us out a table
And spread it with a cloth
Bring us out some mouldy cheese,
And some of your Christmas loaf.

God bless the master of this house
Likewise the mistress too,
And all the little children
That round the table go.

Good master and good mistress
While you're sitting by the fire,
Pray think of us poor children
Who are wandering in the mire.

*Traditional*

# Nowell Sing We

*Nowell sing we, both all and some,*
*Now Rex pacificus is ycome.*
*Exortum est* in love and lysse.
Now Christ his gree he gan us gysse,
And with his body us brought to bliss,
   *Both all and some.*

*De fructu ventris* of Mary bright,
Both God and man in her alight,
Out of disease he did us dight:

*Puer natus* to us was sent,
To bliss us bought, fro bale us blent,
And else to woe we had ywent:

*Lux fulgebit* with love and light,
In Mary mild his pennon pight,
In her took kind with manly might:

*Gloria tibi*, ay, and bliss,
God unto his grace he us wysse,
The rent of heaven that we not miss:

*Nowell sing we, both all and some,*
*Now Rex pacificus is ycome.*

                                        *Traditional*

30

I SING OF A MAIDEN

# I Sing of a Maiden

I sing of a maiden
    That is makèless;
King of all kings
    To her son she ches.

He came all so still
    Where his mother was,
As dew in April
    That falleth on the grass.

He came all so still
    To his mother's bowr,
As dew in April
    That falleth on the flower.

He came all so still
    Where his mother lay,
As dew in April
    That falleth on the spray.

Mother and maiden
    Was never none but she;
Well may such a lady
    Godès mother be.

*Traditional*

# A Virgin Most Pure

A virgin most pure, as the prophets do tell,
Hath brought forth a baby, as it hath befell,
To be our Redeemer from death, hell and sin,
Which Adam's transgression hath wrapped us in.

*Aye, and therefore be you merry,*
*Rejoice and be you merry,*
*Set sorrows aside!*
*Christ Jesus, our Saviour,*
*Was born on this tide.*

In Bethlehem in Jewry a city there was,
Where Joseph and Mary together did pass,
And there to be taxed with many one more,
For Caesar commanded the same should be so.

But when they had entered the city so fair,
The number of people so mighty was there
That Joseph and Mary, whose substance was small,
Could find in the inn there no lodging at all.

Then were they constrained in a stable to lie,
Where horses and asses they used for to tie;
Their lodging so simple they took it no scorn
But against the next morning our Saviour was born.

The King of all kings to this world being brought,
Small store of fine linen to wrap him was sought;
When Mary had swaddled her young Son so sweet,
In an ox's manger she laid him to sleep.

Then God sent an Angel from heaven so high,
To certain poor shepherds in fields where they lie,
And bid them no longer in sorrow to stay,
Because that our Saviour was born on this day.

Then presently after, the shepherds did spy
A number of Angels appear in the sky,
Who joyfully talked, and sweetly did sing,
'To God be the Glory, Our Heavenly King.'

*Traditional*

# The Mother of God

The threefold terror of love; a fallen flare
Through the hollow of an ear;
Wings beating about the room;
The terror of all terrors that I bore
The Heavens in my womb.

Had I not found content among the shows
Every common woman knows,
Chimney corner, garden walk,
Or rocky cistern where we tread the clothes
And gather all the talk?

What is this flesh I purchased with my pains,
This fallen star my milk sustains,
This love that makes my heart's blood stop
Or strikes a sudden chill into my bones
And bids my hair stand up?

*W. B. Yeats (1865–1939)*

# The Cherry Tree Carol

Joseph was an old man,
And an old man was he,
When he wedded Mary
In the land of Galilee.

Joseph and Mary walked
Through an orchard good,
Where was cherries and berries
So red as any blood.

Joseph and Mary walked
Through an orchard green,
Where was berries and cherries
As thick as might be seen.

O then bespoke Mary,
With words so meek and mild,
'Pluck me one cherry, Joseph,
For I am with child.'

O then bespoke Joseph,
With answer most unkind,
'Let him pluck thee a cherry
That brought thee now with child.'

O then bespoke the baby
Within his mother's womb –
'Bow down then the tallest tree
For my mother to have some.'

Then bowed down the highest tree,
Unto his mother's hand.
Then she cried, 'See, Joseph,
I have cherries at command.'

O then bespoke Joseph –
'I have done Mary wrong;
But now cheer up, my dearest,
And do not be cast down.

'O eat your cherries, Mary,
O eat your cherries now,
O eat your cherries, Mary,
That grow upon the bough.'

Then Mary plucked a cherry,
As red as any blood;
Then Mary she went homewards
All with her heavy load.

As Joseph was a-walking,
He heard an angel sing:
'This night there shall be born
On earth our heavenly King.

'He neither shall be born
In housen nor in hall,
Nor in the place of Paradise,
But in an ox's stall.

'He neither shall be clothed
In purple nor in pall,
But all in the fair white linen,
As wear the babies all.

'He neither shall be rocked
In silver nor in gold,
But in a wooden cradle
That rocks upon the mould.

'He neither shall be christened
In white wine nor red,
But with fair spring water
As we were christened.'

Then Mary took her young son,
And set him on her knee;
Saying, 'My dear son, tell me,
Tell me how this world shall be.'

'O I shall be as dead, mother,
As stones are in the wall;
O the stones in the streets, mother,
Shall sorrow for me all.

'On Easter-day dear mother,
My rising up shall be;
O the sun and the moon, mother,
Shall both arise with me.'

*Traditional*

# Joseph

If the stars fell; night's nameless dreams
  Of bliss and blasphemy came true,
If skies were green and snow were gold,
  And you loved me as I love you;

O long light hands and curled brown hair,
  And eyes where sits a naked soul;
Dare I even then draw near and burn
  My fingers in the aureole?

Yes, in the one wise foolish hour
  God gives this strange strength to a man.
He can demand, though not deserve,
  Where ask he cannot, seize he can.

But once the blood's wild wedding o'er,
  Were not dread his, half dark desire,
To see the Christ-child in the cot,
  The Virgin Mary by the fire?

*G. K. Chesterton (1874–1936)*

# The Angel Gabriel

The angel Gabriel from heaven came,
His wings as drifted snow, his eyes as flame:
'All hail,' said he, 'thou lowly maiden Mary'
*Most highly favoured lady! Gloria!*

'For known a blessed Mother thou shalt be;
All generations laud and honour thee:
Thy son shall be Emmanuel, by seers foretold'
*Most highly favoured lady! Gloria!*

Then gentle Mary meekly bowed her head;
'To me be as it pleaseth God!' she said.
'My soul shall laud and magnify his holy Name.'
*Most highly favoured lady! Gloria!*

Of her Emmanuel, the Christ, was born,
In Bethlehem, all on a Christmas morn;
And Christian folk throughout the world will ever say:
*Most highly favoured lady! Gloria!*

*Traditional tr. Sabine Baring-Gould (1834–1924)*

# Once in Royal David's City

Once in Royal David's city
  Stood a lowly cattle shed,
Where a mother laid her Baby
  In a manger for his bed.
Mary was that mother mild,
  Jesus Christ her little child.

He came down from earth to heaven
  Who is God and Lord of All
And his shelter was a stable
  And his cradle was a stall,
With the poor and mean and lowly
  Lived on earth our Saviour holy.

And through all his wondrous childhood
  He would honour and obey
Love, and watch the lowly maiden
  In whose gentle arms he lay.
Christian children all must be
  Mild, obedient, good as he.

For he is our childhood's pattern
  Day by day like us he grew;
He was little, weak and helpless;
  Tears and smiles like us he knew;
And he feeleth for our sadness,
  And he shareth in our gladness.

And our eyes at last shall see him,
  Through his own redeeming love;

For that Child so dear and gentle
  Is our Lord in heaven above;
And he leads his children on
  To the place where he is gone.

Not in that poor lowly stable,
  With the oxen standing by,
We shall see him, but in heaven,
  Set at God's right hand on high,
When, like stars, his children crowned
  All in white shall wait around.

*Cecil Frances Alexander (1818–1895)*

# O Little Town of Bethlehem

O little town of Bethlehem,
  How still we see thee lie!
Above thy deep and dreamless sleep
  The silent stars go by.
Yet in thy dark streets shineth
  The everlasting light
The hopes and fears of all the years
  Are met in thee tonight.

O morning stars, together
  Proclaim the holy birth,
And praises sing to God the King,
  And peace to men on earth;
For Christ is born of Mary;
  And, gathered all above,
While mortals sleep, the angels keep
  Their watch of wondering love.

How silently, how silently,
  The wondrous gift is given!
So God imparts to human hearts
  The blessings of his heaven.
No ear may hear his coming;
  But in this world of sin,
Where meek souls will receive him, still
  The dear Christ enters in.

Where children pure and happy
  Pray to the blessed child,
Where misery cries out to thee,
  Son of the mother mild;

Where charity stands watching
  And faith holds wide the door,
The dark night wakes, the glory breaks,
  And Christmas comes once more.

O holy Child of Bethlehem
  Descend to us we pray;
Cast out our sin, and enter in,
  Be born in us today.
We hear the Christmas angels
  The great glad tidings tell:
O come to us, abide with us;
  Our Lord Emmanuel.

*Phillips Brooks (1835–1893)*

# Away in a Manger

Away in a manger, no crib for a bed,
The little Lord Jesus laid down his sweet head.
The stars in the bright sky looked down where he lay,
The little Lord Jesus asleep on the hay.

The cattle are lowing, the Baby awakes,
But little Lord Jesus no crying he makes.
I love thee, Lord Jesus! look down from the sky,
And stay by my side until morning is nigh.

Be near me, Lord Jesus; I ask thee to stay
Close by me for ever, and love me, I pray.
Bless all the dear children in thy tender care,
And fit us for heaven, to live with thee there.

*Traditional*

# The Old Hark

Hark, hark what news the angels bring:
Glad tidings of a new-born King
Who is the Saviour of mankind
In whom we shall salvation find.

This the day; this blessed morn
The Saviour of mankind was born;
Born of a maid, a virgin pure,
Born without sin, from guilt secure.

Hail, blessed Virgin, full of grace!
Blessed above all mortal race,
Whose blessed womb brought forth in one,
A God, a Saviour, and a Son.

A perfect God, a perfect man,
A mystery which no man can
Attain to, though he's e'er so wise,
Till he ascend above the skies.

Arise, my soul, and then, my voice,
In hymns of praise early rejoice,
His fame extol and magnify,
Upon these errands Angels fly.

As angels sung at Jesus' birth,
Sure we have greater cause for mirth;
For why? It was for our sake
Christ did our human nature take.

Dear Christ, Thou didst Thyself debase,
Thus to descend to human race,
And leave Thy Father's throne above,
Lord, what could move Thee to this love?

Man that was made out of the dust,
He found a paradise at first;
But see the God of Heaven and earth
Laid in a manger at his birth.

Surely the manger where he lies
Doth figure out his sacrifice,
And by his birth all men may see
A pattern of humility.

Stupendous Babe! my God and King,
Thy praises I will ever sing,
In joyful accents raise my voice,
And in my praise of God rejoice.

My soul, learn by thy Saviour's birth
For to debase thyself on earth,
That I may be exalted high,
To live with him eternally.

I am resolved whilst here I live,
As I'm in duty bound, to give
All glory to the Deity,
One God alone, in persons three.

*Traditional*

48

# Angels, from the Realms of Glory

Angels, from the realms of glory,
  Wing your flight o'er all the earth;
Ye who sang creation's story,
  Now proclaim Messiah's birth:

*Come and worship, come and worship,*
  *Worship Christ, the new-born King.*

Shepherds, in the field abiding
  Watching o'er your flocks by night,
God with man is now residing,
  Yonder shines the infant Light:

Sages, leave your contemplations:
  Brighter visions beam afar:
Seek the great Desire of Nations;
  Ye have seen his natal star:

Saints before the altar bending,
  Watching long in hope and fear,
Suddenly the Lord, descending,
  In his temple shall appear:

Sinners, wrung with keen repentance,
  Doomed for guilt to endless pains;
Justice now repeals the sentence,
  Mercy calls you – break your chains.

*James Montgomery (1771–1854)*

# Hark! The Herald Angels Sing

Hark! the herald angels sing
   Glory to the new-born King,
Peace on earth and mercy mild,
   God and sinners reconciled.
Joyful all ye nations rise,
   Join the triumph of the skies;
With th'angelic host proclaim:
   'Christ is born in Bethlehem.'
Hark! the herald angels sing
   Glory to the new-born King.

Christ, by highest Heav'n adored,
   Christ, the Everlasting Lord,
Late in time behold him come,
   Offspring of a virgin's womb.
Veiled in flesh the Godhead see,
   Hail the incarnate Deity!
Pleased as Man with man to dwell,
   Jesus, our Emmanuel.
Hark! the herald angels sing
   Glory to the new-born King.

Hail, the heaven-born Prince of Peace!
   Hail, the Sun of Righteousness!
Light and life to all he brings,
   Risen with healing in his wings.
Mild he lays his glory by,
   Born that man no more may die,

Born to raise the sons of earth,
  Born to give them second birth.
Hark! the herald angels sing
  Glory to the new-born King.

*Charles Wesley* (1707–1788)

# A Hymn for Christmas Day

Arise, and hail the sacred day!
Cast all low cares of life away,
And thought of meaner things;
This day, to cure thy deadly woes,
The Sun of Righteousness arose
With healing in His wings.

If Angels on that happy morn
The Saviour of the world was born,
Poured forth seraphic songs;
Much more should we of human race
Adore the wonders of His grace,
To whom that grace belongs.

How wonderful, how vast His love,
Who left the shining realms above,
Those happy seats of rest;
How much for lost mankind He bore,
Their peace and pardon to restore,
Can never be expressed.

While we adore His boundless grace,
And pious joy and mirth take place
Of sorrow, grief, and pain,
Give glory to our God on high,
And not among the general joy
Forget good-will to men.

O then let Heaven and earth rejoice,
Creation's whole united voice,

And hymn the Sacred Day,
When sin and Satan vanquished fell,
And all the powers of death and hell,
Before His sovereign sway.

*Traditional*

# Joy to the World!

Joy to the world! the Lord is come:
  Let earth receive her King!
Let ev'ry heart prepare him room,
And heav'n and nature sing!
And heav'n and nature sing!
And heav'n and heav'n and nature sing!

Joy to the earth! the Saviour reigns:
  Let men their songs employ,
While fields and floods, rocks, hills and plains
Repeat the sounding joy.
Repeat the sounding joy.
Repeat, repeat the sounding joy.

No more let sins and sorrows grow,
  Nor thorns infest the ground:
He comes to make his blessings flow
Far as the curse is found.
Far as the curse is found.
Far as, far as the curse is found.

He rules the world with truth and grace,
  And makes the nations prove
The glories of his righteousness
And wonders of his love.
And wonders of his love.
And wonders and wonders of his love.

*Isaac Watts (1674–1748)*

54

# In Dulci Jubilo

*In dulci jubilo*
   Let us our homage show:
   Our heart's joy reclineth
*In praesepio*;
   And like a bright star shineth
*Matris in gremio*.
*Alpha es et O!*

*O Jesu parvule*,
   My heart is sore for Thee!
   Hear me, I beseech Thee,
*O puer optime*;
   My praying let it reach Thee!
*O princeps gloriae*.
*Trahe me post te*.

*O patris caritas!*
   *O Nati lenitas!*
   Deeply were we stained
*Per nostra crimina*;
   But Thou for us hast gained
*Coelorum gaudia*.
*Qualis gloria!*

*Ubi sunt gaudia*,
   If that they be not there?
   There are Angels singing
*Nova cantica*;
   And there the bells are ringing
*In Regis curia*.
   O that we were there!

*Traditional*

# Christmas – A Song of Joy at Dawn

All my heart this night rejoices,
　　As I hear, far and near,
　　Sweetest angel voices:
'Christ is born,' their choirs are singing,
　　Till the air, everywhere,
　　Now with joy is ringing.

Hark! a voice from yonder manger
　　Soft and sweet, doth entreat,
　　'Flee from woe and danger!
Brethren, come from all doth grieve you
　　You are freed; all you need,
　　I will surely give you.'

For it dawns, the promised morrow
　　Of His birth, who the earth
　　Rescues from her sorrow.
God to wear our form descendeth,
　　Of His grace to our race
　　Here His Son he lendeth.

Come, then, let us hasten yonder!
　　Here let all, great and small,
　　Kneel in awe and wonder!
Love Him who with love is yearning:
　　Hail the star that from far
　　Bright with hope is burning.

Yea, so truly for us careth,
　　That His Son all we've done
　　As our offering beareth;

As our Lamb who, dying for us,
   Bears our load, and to God
   Doth in peace restore us.

Ye who pine in weary sadness,
   Weep no more, for the door
   Now is found of gladness.
Cling to Him, for He will guide you
   Where no cross, pain or loss
   Can again betide you.

Hither come, ye heavy-hearted;
   Who for sin deep within,
   Long and fore have smarted;
For the poisoned wounds you're feeling
   Help is near, One is here
   Mighty for their healing!

Hither come, ye poor and wretched;
   Know His will is to fill
   Every hand outstretched;
Here are riches without measure,
   Here forget all regret,
   Fill your hearts with treasure.

Blessed Saviour, let me find Thee!
   Keep Thou me close to Thee,
   Cast me not behind Thee!
Life of life, my heart Thou stillest,
   Calm I rest on Thy breast,
   All this void Thou fillest.

*Traditional*

# O Come, All Ye Faithful

O come, all ye faithful,
Joyful and triumphant,
O come ye, O come ye to Bethlehem;
Come and behold him
Born the King of angels.

> *O come, let us adore him,*
> *O come, let us adore him,*
> *O come, let us adore him,*
> *Christ the Lord.*

God of God,
Light of Light,
Lo! he abhors not the Virgin's womb;
Very God,
Begotten, not created.

See how the shepherds
Summoned to his cradle,
Leaving their flocks, draw nigh to gaze!
We, too, will thither
Bend our hearts' oblations.

Lo, star-led chieftains,
Magi, Christ adoring,
Offer him incense, gold and myrrh;
We to the Christ-child
Bring our hearts' oblations.

Child, for us sinners,
Poor and in the manger,
Fain we embrace thee with love and awe:
Who would not love thee,
Loving us so dearly?

Sing, choirs of angels!
Sing in exultation!
Sing, all ye citizens of heaven above:
'Glory to God
In the highest.'

Yea, Lord we greet thee,
Born this happy morning;
Jesu, to thee be glory given
Word of the Father
Now in flesh appearing.

*Traditional tr. F. Oakeley and W. T. Brooke*
*(1802–1880 and 1848–1917)*

# PEACE AND LULLABIES

# Peace

My soul, there is a country
  Far beyond the stars,
Where stands a wingèd sentry
  All skilful in the wars.
There, above noise and danger,
  Sweet peace sits crown'd with smiles,
And one born in a manger
  Commands the beauteous files.
He is thy gracious friend
  And (O my soul, awake!)
Did in pure love descend
  To die here for thy sake.
If thou canst get but thither,
  There grows the flower of peace,
The rose that cannot wither,
  Thy fortress, and thy ease.
Leave then thy foolish ranges;
  For none can thee secure
But one, who never changes,
  Thy God, thy life, thy cure.

*Henry Vaughan (1622–1695)*

# A Child this Day is Born

A child this day is born,
  A child of high renown,
Most worthy of a sceptre,
  A sceptre and a crown:

   *Nowell, Nowell, Nowell,*
    *Nowell, sing all we may,*
   *Because the King of all kings*
    *Was born this blessed day.*

These tidings shepherds heard,
  In field watching their fold,
Were by an angel unto them
  That night revealed and told:

To whom the angel spoke,
  Saying, 'Be not afraid;
Be glad, poor silly shepherds –
  Why are you so dismayed?

'For lo! I bring you tidings
  Of gladness and of mirth,
Which cometh to all people by
  This holy infant's birth':

Then was there with the angel
  An host incontinent
Of heavenly bright soldiers,
  Which from the Highest was sent:

Lauding the Lord our God,
  And his celestial King;
All glory be in Paradise,
  This heavenly host did sing:

And as the angel told them,
  So to them did appear;
They found the young child, Jesus Christ,
  With Mary, his mother dear:

  *Nowell, Nowell, Nowell,*
    *Nowell, sing all we may,*
  *Because the King of all kings*
    *Was born this blessed day.*

                              *Traditional*

# Silent Night

Silent night, holy night,
All is calm, all is bright
Round yon virgin mother and child.
Holy infant, so tender and mild,
Sleep in heavenly peace.
Sleep in heavenly peace.

Silent night, holy night,
Shepherds quake at the sight,
Glories stream from heaven afar,
Heavenly hosts sing alleluia;
Christ, the Savior, is born!
Christ, the Savior, is born!

Silent night, holy night,
Son of God, love's pure light
Radiant beams from thy holy face,
With the dawn of redeeming grace,
Jesus, Lord, at thy birth.
Jesus, Lord, at thy birth.

*Joseph Mohr tr. John Freeman Young*
*(1792–1848 and 1820–1885)*

# Christus Natus Est

In Bethlehem
On Christmas morn,
The lowly gem
Of love was born.
Hosannah! *Christus natus est.*

Bright in her crown
Of fiery star,
Judea's town
Shone from afar:
Hosannah! *Christus natus est.*

While beasts in stall,
On bended knee,
Did carol all
Most joyously:
Hosannah! *Christus natus est.*

For bird and beast
He did not come,
But for the least
Of mortal scum.
Hosannah! *Christus natus est.*

Who lies in ditch?
Who begs his bread?
Who has no stitch
For back or head?
Hosannah! *Christus natus est.*

Who wakes to weep,
Lies down to mourn?
Who in his sleep
Withdraws from scorn?
Hosannah! *Christus natus est.*

Ye outraged dust,
On field and plain,
To feed the lust
Of madmen slain:
Hosannah! *Christus natus est.*

The manger still
Outshines the throne;
Christ must and will
Come to his own.
Hosannah! *Christus natus est.*

*Countee Cullen (1903–1946)*

# On Christmas Day to My Heart

To Day
Hark! Heaven sings!
Stretch, tune my Heart
(For hearts have strings
May bear their part)
And though thy Lute were bruis'd i' th' fall;
Bruis'd hearts may reach an humble Pastoral.

To Day
Shepheards rejoyce
And Angells do
No more: thy voice
Can reach that too:
Bring then at least thy pipe along
And mingle Consort with the Angells Song.

To Day
A shed that's thatch'd
(Yet straws can sing)
Holds God; God's match'd
With beasts; Beasts bring
Their song their way; For shame then raise
Thy notes; Lambs bleat and Oxen bellow Praise.

To Day
God honour'd Man
Not Angells: Yet
They sing; And can
Rais'd Man forget?
Praise is our debt to-day, nor shall
Angells (Man's not so poor) discharge it all.

To Day
Then screwe thee high
My Heart: Up to
The Angells key;
Sing Glory; Do;
What if thy stringes all crack and flye?
On such a Ground, Musick 'twill be to dy.

*Clement Paman (1612–1663)*

# An Ode of the Birth of Our Saviour

In Numbers, and but these few,
I sing Thy Birth, Oh JESU!
Thou prettie Babie, borne here,
With sup'rabundant scorn here:
Who for Thy Princely Port here,
      Hadst for Thy place
      Of Birth, a base
Out-stable for thy Court here.

Instead of neat Inclosures
Of inter-woven Osiers;
Instead of fragrant Posies
Of Daffadills, and Roses;
Thy cradle, Kingly Stranger,
      As Gospell tells,
      Was nothing els,
But, here, a homely manger.

But we with Silks, (not Cruells)
With sundry precious Jewells,
And Lilly-work will dresse Thee;
And as we dispossesse thee
Of clouts, wee'l make a chamber,
      Sweet Babe, for Thee,
      Of Ivorie,
And plaister'd round with Amber.

The Jewes they did disdaine Thee,
But we will entertaine Thee

With Glories to await here
Upon Thy Princely State here,
And more for love, then pittie.
            From yeere to yeere
            Wee'l make Thee, here,
A Free-born of our Citie.

*Robert Herrick (1591–1674)*

# The House of Christmas

There fared a mother driven forth
Out of an inn to roam;
In the place where she was homeless
All men are at home.
The crazy stable close at hand,
With shaking timber and shifting sand,
Grew a stronger thing to abide and stand
Than the square stones of Rome.

For men are homesick in their homes,
And strangers under the sun,
And they lay their heads in a foreign land
Whenever the day is done.
Here we have battle and blazing eyes,
And chance and honour and high surprise,
But our homes are under miraculous skies
Where the yule tale was begun.

A Child in a foul stable,
Where the beasts feed and foam;
Only where He was homeless
Are you and I at home;
We have hands that fashion and heads that know,
But our hearts we lost – how long ago!
In a place no chart nor ship can show
Under the sky's dome.

This world is wild as an old wives' tale,
And strange the plain things are,
The earth is enough and the air is enough
For our wonder and our war;

But our rest is as far as the fire-drake swings
And our peace is put in impossible things
Where clashed and thundered unthinkable wings
Round an incredible star.

To an open house in the evening
Home shall men come,
To an older place than Eden
And a taller town than Rome.
To the end of the way of the wandering star,
To the things that cannot be and that are,
To the place where God was homeless
And all men are at home.

*G. K. Chesterton (1874–1936)*

# The Nativity of Our Lord
# and Saviour Jesus Christ

Where is this stupendous stranger?
  Swains of Solyma, advise;
Lead me to my Master's manger,
  Shew me where my Saviour lies.

O Most Mighty! O MOST HOLY!
  Far beyond the seraph's thought,
Art thou then so mean and lowly
  As unheeded prophets taught?

O the magnitude of meekness!
  Worth from worth immortal sprung;
O the strength of infant weakness,
  If eternal is so young!

If so young and thus eternal,
  Michael tune the shepherd's reed,
Where the scenes are ever vernal,
  And the loves be love indeed!

See the God blasphem'd and doubted
  In the schools of Greece and Rome;
See the pow'rs of darkness routed,
  Taken at their utmost gloom.

Nature's decorations glisten
  Far above their usual trim;
Birds on box and laurels listen,
  As so near the cherubs hymn.

Boreas now no longer winters
  On the desolated coast;
Oaks no more are riv'n in splinters
  By the whirlwind and his host.

Spinks and ouzles sing sublimely,
  'We too have a Saviour born';
Whiter blossoms burst untimely
  On the blest Mosaic thorn.

God all-bounteous, all-creative,
  Whom no ills from good dissuade,
Is incarnate, and a native
  Of the very world he made.

                    *Christopher Smart (1722–1771)*

# New Prince, New Pomp

Behold, a silly tender Babe
  In freezing winter night
In homely manger trembling lies,
  Alas, a piteous sight!

The inns are full; no man will yield
  This little pilgrim bed,
But forced he is with silly beasts
  In crib to shroud his head.

Despise him not for lying there,
  First, what he is inquire;
An orient pearl is often found
  In depth of dirty mire.

Weigh not his crib, his wooden dish,
  Nor beasts that by him feed;
Weigh not his Mother's poor attire,
  Nor Joseph's simple weed.

This stable is a Prince's court,
  This crib his chair of state;
The beasts are parcel of his pomp,
  The wooden dish his plate.

The persons in that poor attire
  His royal liveries wear;
The Prince himself is come from heaven;
  This pomp is prized there.

With joy approach, O Christian wight,
  Do homage to thy King;
And highly praise his humble pomp,
  Which he from heaven doth bring.

*Robert Southwell (c.1561–1595)*

# Past Three O'Clock

*Past three o'clock*
*And a cold frosty morning:*
*Past three o'clock:*
*Good morrow, masters all!*

Born is a Baby
Gentle as may be,
Son of th' eternal
Father supernal.

Seraph quire singeth,
Angel bell ringeth,
Hark how they rime it,
time it and chime it!

Mid earth rejoices
Hearing such voices
Ne'ertofore so well
Carolling 'Nowell'.

Hinds o'er the pearly,
Dewy lawn early
Seek the high stranger
Laid in the manger.

Cheese from the dairy
Bring they for Mary,
And, nor for money,
Butter and honey.

Light out of star-land
Leadeth from far land
Princes to meet him,
Worship and greet him.

Myrrh for full coffer,
Incense they offer;
Nor is the golden
Nugget withholden.

Thus they: I pray you,
Up, sirs, nor stay you
Till ye confess him
Likewise, and bless him.

*George Ratcliffe Woodward*
*(1848–1934)*

# Love Came Down at Christmas

Love came down at Christmas,
  Love all lovely, Love Divine;
Love was born at Christmas,
  Star and angels gave the sign.

Worship we the Godhead,
  Love Incarnate, Love Divine;
Worship we our Jesus:
  But wherewith for sacred sign?

Love shall be our token,
  Love be yours and love be mine,
Love to God and all men,
  Love for plea and gift and sign.

*Christina Rossetti (1830–1894)*

# Before the Paling of the Stars

Before the paling of the stars,
  Before the winter morn,
  Before the earliest cock-crow,
Jesus Christ was born:
    Born in a stable,
  Cradled in a manger,
In the world his hands had made
  Born a stranger.

Priest and King lay fast asleep
  In Jerusalem;
Young and old lay fast asleep
  In crowded Bethlehem;
Saint and Angel, ox and ass,
  Kept a watch together,
  Before the Christmas daybreak
  In the winter weather.

Jesus on His Mother's breast
  In the stable cold,
Spotless Lamb of God was He,
  Shepherd of the fold:
Let us kneel with Mary Maid
  With Joseph bent and hoary,
With Saint and Angel, ox and ass,
  To hail the King of Glory.

*Christina Rossetti (1830–1894)*

# The Coventry Carol

*Lully, lullay, thou little tiny child,*
*By by, lully, lullay, thou little tiny child,*
*By by, lully, lullay.*

O sisters too, how may we do
For to preserve this day
This poor youngling for whom we do sing,
By by, lully lullay?

Herod the king, in his raging,
Charged he hath this day
His men of might, in his own sight,
All young children to slay.

Then woe is me, poor child for thee!
And ever mourn and say,
For thy parting neither say nor sing
By by, lully, lullay.

*Traditional*

# A Christmas Carol

The Christ-child lay on Mary's lap,
  His hair was like a light.
(O weary, weary were the world,
  But here is all aright.)

The Christ-child lay on Mary's breast,
  His hair was like a star.
(O stern and cunning are the kings,
  But here the true hearts are.)

The Christ-child lay on Mary's heart,
  His hair was like a fire.
(O weary, weary is the world,
  But here the world's desire.)

The Christ-child stood at Mary's knee,
  His hair was like a crown,
And all the flowers looked up at him,
  And all the stars looked down.

*G. K. Chesterton (1874–1936)*

# A Cradle Song

Sweet dreams form a shade
O'er my lovely infant's head:
Sweet dreams of pleasant streams
By happy, silent moony beams.

Sweet sleep with soft down
Weave thy brows an infant crown;
Sweet sleep, angel mild,
Hover o'er my happy child.

Sweet smiles in the night,
Hover over my delight;
Sweet smiles, mother's smiles,
All the livelong night beguiles.

Sweet moans, dovelike sighs,
Chase not slumber from thy eyes;
Sweet moans, sweeter smiles,
All the dovelike moans beguiles.

Sleep, sleep, happy child;
All creation slept and smiled;
Sleep, sleep, happy sleep,
While o'er thee thy mother weep.

Sweet babe, in thy face
Holy image I can trace:
Sweet babe, once like thee
Thy Maker lay and wept for me.

Wept for me, for thee, for all
When He was an infant small:
Thou His image ever see,
Heavenly face that smiles on thee.

Smiles on me, on thee, on all,
Who became an infant small:
Infant smiles are His own smiles,
Heaven and earth to peace beguiles.

*William Blake (1757–1827)*

# The Rocking Carol

Little Jesus, sweetly sleep, do not stir;
We will lend a coat of fur,
  We will rock you, rock you, rock you,
  We will rock you, rock you, rock you:
See the fur to keep you warm
Snugly round your tiny form.

Mary's little baby, sleep, sweetly sleep,
Sleep in comfort, slumber deep,
  We will rock you, rock you, rock you,
  We will rock you, rock you, rock you:
We will serve you all we can,
Darling, darling little man.

*Percy Dearmer (1867–1936)*

# Infant Holy

Infant holy,
Infant lowly,
For his bed a cattle stall;
Oxen lowing,
Little knowing
Christ the babe is Lord of all.
Swift are winging,
Angels singing,
Nowells ringing,
Tidings bringing,
Christ the babe is Lord of all,
Christ the babe is Lord of all.

Flocks were sleeping,
Shepherds keeping
Vigil till the morning new
Saw the glory,
Heard the story,
Tidings of a gospel true.
Thus rejoicing,
Free from sorrow,
Praises voicing,
Greet the morrow,
Christ the babe was born for you!
Christ the babe was born for you!

*Traditional tr. Edith M. G. Reed*
*(1885–1933)*

# Sing Lullaby

Sing lullaby!
Lullaby baby, now reclining:
　　Sing lullaby!
Hush, do not wake the infant king;
Angels are watching, stars are shining
Over the place where he is lying:
　　Sing lullaby.

　　Sing lullaby!
Lullaby baby, sweetly sleeping:
　　Sing lullaby!
Hush, do not wake the infant king;
Soon will come sorrow with the morning,
Soon will come bitter grief and weeping:
　　Sing lullaby!

　　Sing lullaby!
Lullaby, baby, gently dozing:
　　Sing lullaby!
Hush, do not wake the infant king;
Soon comes the cross, the nails, the piercing,
Then in the grave at last reposing:
　　Sing lullaby!

　　Sing lullaby!
Lullaby! Is the baby waking?
　　Sing lullaby!
Hush, do not stir the infant king,

Dreaming of Easter, gladsome morning,
Conquering death, its bondage breaking:
  Sing lullaby!

*Sabine Baring-Gould*
*(1834–1924)*

# Welcome to Heaven's King

Welcome to Thou, Heaven's King,
Welcome, born in one morning,
Welcome, for Him we shall sing,
  Welcome, Yule!

*Traditional*

# Hymn for Christmas Day

Christians awake, salute the happy morn,
Whereon the Saviour of the world was born;
Rise, to adore the mystery of love,
Which hosts of angels chanted from above:
With them the joyful tidings first begun
Of God incarnate, and the Virgin's son.
Then to the watchful shepherds it was told,
Who heard the angelic herald's voice: 'Behold!
I bring good tidings of a Saviour's birth
To you, and all the nations upon earth!
This day hath God fulfilled his promised Word;
This day is born a Saviour, Christ, the Lord.
In David's city, shepherds, ye shall find
The long foretold redeemer of mankind;
Wrapped up in swaddling clothes, the babe divine
Lies in a manger: this shall be your sign.'
He spake, and straightway the celestial choir,
In hymns of joy unknown before, conspire;
The praises of redeeming love they sung,
And heaven's whole orb with hallelujahs rung.
God's highest glory was their anthem still;
Peace upon earth, and mutual good will.
To Bethlehem straight the enlightened shepherds ran,
To see the wonder God had wrought for man;
And found, with Joseph and the blessed maid,
Her Son, the Saviour, in a manger laid.
Amazed, the wondrous story they proclaim –
The first apostles of His infant fame;
While Mary keeps, and ponders in her heart,
The heavenly vision which the swains impart.

They to their flocks, still praising God, return,
And their glad hearts within their bosoms burn.
Let us, like these good shepherds then, employ
Our grateful voices to proclaim the joy;
Like Mary, let us ponder in our mind
God's wondrous love in saving lost mankind;
Artless and watchful as these favoured swains,
While virgin meekness in the heart remains:
Trace we the babe, who has retrieved our loss,
From His poor manger to His bitter cross;
Treading His steps, assisted by His grace,
Till man's first heavenly state again takes place.
Then may we hope the angelic thrones among
To sing, redeemed, a glad triumphal song.
He that was born upon this joyful day
Around us all His glory shall display;
Saved by His love, incessant we shall sing
Of angels, and of angel-men, the King.

*John Byrom (1692–1763)*

# It Was on Christmas Day

It was on Christmas Day,
And all in the morning,
Our Saviour was born,
And our heavenly King:
*And was not this a joyful thing?*
*And sweet Jesus they called him by name.*

*Traditional*

# I Saw a Stable

I saw a stable, low and very bare,
  A little child in a manger.
The oxen knew Him, had Him in their care,
  To men He was a stranger.
The safety of the world was lying there,
  And the world's danger.

*Mary Elizabeth Coleridge (1861–1907)*

# HOLLY AND IVY

# Holly

But give me holly, bold and jolly,
Honest, prickly, shining holly;
Pluck me holly leaf and berry
For the day when I make merry.

*Christina Rossetti (1830–1894)*

# Advent

Earth grown old, yet still so green,
  Deep beneath her crust of cold
Nurses fire unfelt, unseen:
  Earth grown old.

  We who live are quickly told:
Millions more lie hid between
  Inner swathings of her fold.

When will fire break up her screen?
  When will life burst thro' her mould?
Earth, earth, earth, thy cold is keen,
  Earth grown old.

*Christina Rossetti (1830–1894)*

# Green Grow'th the Holly

Green grow'th the holly,
So doth the ivy;
  Though winter blasts blow ne'er so high,
Green grow'th the holly.

Gay are the flowers,
Hedgerows and ploughlands;
  The days grow longer in the sun,
Soft fall the showers.

Full gold the harvest,
Grain for thy labour;
  With God must work for daily bread,
Else, man, thou starvest.

Fast fall the shed leaves,
Russet and yellow;
  But resting-buds are snug and safe
Where swung the dead leaves.

Green grow'th the holly,
So doth the ivy;
  The God of life can never die,
Hope! saith the holly.

*Traditional*

# Lo, How a Rose E'er Blooming

Lo, how a Rose e'er blooming
From tender stem hath sprung!
Of Jesse's lineage coming
As seers of old have sung.
It came, a blossom bright,
Amid the cold of winter,
When half spent was the night.

Isaiah 'twas foretold it,
The Rose I have in mind,
With Mary we behold it,
The Virgin Mother kind.
To show God's love aright,
She bore to us a Savior,
When half spent was the night.

O Flower, whose fragrance tender
With sweetness fills the air,
Dispel in glorious splendor
The darkness everywhere;
True man, yet very God,
From sin and death now save us,
And share our every load.

*Traditional tr. Theodore Baker*
*and Harriet R. K. Spaeth*
*(1851–1934 and 1845–1925)*

# The Mahogany Tree

Christmas is here:
Winds whistle shrill.
Icy and chill:
Little care we.
Little we fear
Weather without,
Sheltered about
The Mahogany Tree.

Commoner greens,
Ivy and oaks,
Poets, in jokes,
Sing, do you see:
Good fellows' shins
Here, boys, are found,
Twisting around
The Mahogany Tree.

Once on the boughs
Birds of rare plume
Sang, in its bloom:
Night birds are we;
Here we carouse,
Singing, like them,
Perched round the stem
Of the jolly old tree.

Here let us sport,
Boys, as we sit:
Laughter and wit
Flashing so free.
Life is but short –
When we are gone,
Let them sing on,
Round the old tree.

Evenings we knew,
Happy as this;
Faces we miss,
Pleasant to see.
Kind hearts and true,
Gentle and just,
Peace to your dust!
We sing round the tree.

Care, like a dun,
Lurks at the gate:
Let the dog wait;
Happy we'll be!
Drink every one;
Pile up the coals,
Fill the red bowls,
Round the old tree!

Drain we the cup. –
Friend, art afraid?
Spirits are laid
In the Red Sea.
Mantle it up;
Empty it yet;
Let us forget,
Round the old tree.

Sorrows, begone!
Life and its ills,
Duns and their bills,
Bid we to flee.
Come with the dawn
Blue-devil sprite,
Leave us to-night,
Round the old tree.

*William Makepeace Thackeray (1811–1863)*

# The Holly and the Ivy

The holly and the ivy,
When they are both full grown,
Of all the trees that are in the wood,
The holly bears the crown.

*The rising of the sun*
*And the running of the deer,*
*The playing of the merry organ,*
*Sweet singing in the choir.*

The holly bears a blossom
As white as lily flower,
And Mary bore sweet Jesus Christ
To be our sweet Saviour.

The holly bears a berry
As red as any blood,
And Mary bore sweet Jesus Christ
To do poor sinners good.

The holly bears a prickle
As sharp as any thorn,
And Mary bore sweet Jesus Christ
On Christmas Day in the morn.

The holly bears a bark
As bitter as any gall,
And Mary bore sweet Jesus Christ
For to redeem us all.

The holly and the ivy,
When they are both full grown,
Of all the trees that are in the wood,
The holly bears the crown.

*Traditional*

# The First Tree in the Greenwood

Now the holly bears a berry as white as the milk,
And Mary bore Jesus, who was wrapped up in silk:
   *And Mary bore Jesus Christ,*
   *Our Saviour for to be,*
   *And the first tree in the greenwood, it was the holly.*

Now the holly bears a berry as green as the grass,
And Mary bore Jesus, who died on the cross:
   *And Mary bore Jesus Christ,*
   *Our Saviour for to be,*
   *And the first tree in the greenwood, it was the holly.*

Now the holly bears a berry as black as the coal,
And Mary bore Jesus, who died for us all:
   *And Mary bore Jesus Christ,*
   *Our Saviour for to be,*
   *And the first tree in the greenwood, it was the holly.*

Now the holly bears a berry, as blood is it red,
Then trust we our Saviour, who rose from the dead:
   *And Mary bore Jesus Christ,*
   *Our Saviour for to be,*
   *And the first tree in the greenwood, it was the holly.*

*Traditional*

# BIRDS AND BEASTS

# Eddi's Service

Eddi, priest of St Wilfrid
  In the chapel at Manhood End,
Ordered a midnight service
  For such as cared to attend.

But the Saxons were keeping Christmas,
  And the night was stormy as well.
Nobody came to service,
  Though Eddi rang the bell.

'Wicked weather for walking,'
  Said Eddi of Manhood End.
'But I must go on with the service
  For such as care to attend.'

The altar-lamps were lighted, –
  An old marsh-donkey came,
Bold as a guest invited,
  And stared at the guttering flame.

The storm beat on at the windows,
  The water splashed on the floor,
And a wet, yoke-weary bullock
  Pushed in through the open door.

'How do I know what is greatest,
  How do I know what is least?
That is my Father's business,'
  Said Eddi, Wilfrid's priest.

'But – three are gathered together –
    Listen to me and attend.
I bring good news, my brethren!'
    Said Eddi, of Manhood End.

And he told the Ox of a manger,
    And a stall in Bethlehem,
And he spoke to the Ass of a Rider
    That rode to Jerusalem.

They steamed and dripped in the chancel,
    They listened and never stirred,
While, just as though they were Bishops,
    Eddi preached them The Word.

Till the gale blew off on the marshes
    And the windows showed the day,
And the Ox and the Ass together
    Wheeled and clattered away.

And when the Saxons mocked him,
    Said Eddi of Manhood End,
'I dare not shut His chapel
    On such as care to attend.'

                    *Rudyard Kipling (1865–1936)*

# The Oxen

Christmas Eve, and twelve of the clock.
'Now they are all on their knees,'
An elder said as we sat in a flock
By the embers in hearthside ease.

We pictured the meek mild creatures where
They dwelt in their strawy pen,
Nor did it occur to one of us there
To doubt they were kneeling then.

So fair a fancy few would weave
In these years! Yet, I feel,
If someone said on Christmas Eve,
'Come; see the oxen kneel

'In the lonely barton by yonder coomb
Our childhood used to know,'
I should go with him in the gloom,
Hoping it might be so.

*Thomas Hardy (1840–1928)*

# Sheep in Winter

The sheep get up and make their many tracks
And bear a load of snow upon their backs,
And gnaw the frozen turnip to the ground
With sharp quick bite, and then go noising round
The boy that pecks the turnips all the day
And knocks his hands to keep the cold away
And laps his legs in straw to keep them warm
And hides behind the hedges from the storm.
The sheep, as tame as dogs, go where he goes
And try to shake their fleeces from the snows,
Then leave their frozen meal and wander round
The stubble stack that stands beside the ground,
And lie all night and face the drizzling storm
And shun the hovel where they might be warm.

*John Clare (1793–1864)*

# While Shepherds Watched Their Flocks

While shepherds watched their flocks by night,
All seated on the ground,
The angel of the Lord came down,
And glory shone around.

'Fear not,' said he (for mighty dread
Had seized their troubled mind);
'Glad tidings of great joy I bring
To you and all mankind.

'To you in David's town this day
Is born of David's line
A Saviour, who is Christ the Lord;
And this shall be the sign:

'The heavenly Babe you there shall find
To human view displayed,
All meanly wrapped in swathing bands,
And in a manger laid.'

Thus spake the seraph; and forthwith
Appeared a shining throng
Of angels praising God, who thus
Addressed their joyful song;

'All glory be to God on high,
And to the earth be peace;
Good will henceforth from heaven to men
Begin and never cease.'

*Nahum Tate (1652–1715)*

# Go, Tell it on the Mountain

*Go, tell it on the mountain,*
*Over the hills and ev'rywhere:*
*Go, tell it on the mountain*
*That Jesus Christ is born.*

While shepherds kept their watching
 O'er silent flocks by night,
Behold, throughout the heavens
 There shone a holy light:

The shepherds feared and trembled
 When, lo, above the earth
Rang out the angel chorus
 That hailed our Saviour's birth:

And lo! When they had seen it
 They all bowed down and prayed;
They travelled on together
 To where the babe was laid.

Down in a lonely manger
 The humble Christ was born;
And God sent us salvation
 That blessed Christmas morn.

*Traditional*

# The Shepherds' Carol

We stood on the hills, Lady,
Our day's work done,
Watching the frosted meadows
That winter had won.

The evening was calm, Lady,
The air so still.
Silence more lovely than music
Folded the hill.

There was a star, Lady,
Shone in the night,
Larger than Venus it was
And bright, so bright,

Oh, a voice from the sky, Lady,
It seemed to us then
Telling of God being born
In the world of men.

And so we have come, Lady,
Our day's work done.
Our love, our hopes, ourselves
We give to your son.

*Traditional*

# Out in the Dark

Out in the dark over the snow
The fallow fawns invisible go
With the fallow doe;
And the winds blow
Fast as the stars are slow.

Stealthily the dark haunts round
And, when the lamp goes, without sound
At a swifter bound
Than the swiftest hound,
Arrives, and all else is drowned;

And star and I and wind and deer,
Are in the dark together, – near,
Yet far, – and fear
Drums on my ear
In the sage company drear.

How weak and little is the light,
All the universe of sight,
Love and delight,
Before the might,
If you love it not, of night.

Edward Thomas (1878–1917)

# Birds at Winter Nightfall

Around the house the flakes fly faster,
And all the berries now are gone
From holly and cotoneaster
Around the house. The flakes fly! – faster
Shutting indoors that crumb-outcaster
We used to see upon the lawn
Around the house. The flakes fly faster,
And all the berries now are gone!

*Thomas Hardy (1840–1928)*

# Little Robin Redbreast

Little Robin Redbreast
Sat upon a tree,
He sang merrily,
As merrily as could be.
He nodded with his head,
And his tail waggled he,
As little Robin Redbreast
Sat upon a tree.

*Traditional*

SNOW AND ICE

# Christmas Night

Softly, softly, through the darkness
　　Snow is falling.
Sharply, sharply, in the meadows
　　Lambs are calling.
Coldly, coldly, all around me
　　Winds are blowing.
Brightly, brightly, up above me
　　Stars are glowing.

*Traditional*

# The First Nowell

The first Nowell the angel did say
Was to certain poor shepherds in fields as they lay;
In fields where they lay, keeping their sheep,
In a cold winter's night that was so deep:
*Nowell, Nowell, Nowell, Nowell,*
*Born is the King of Israel!*

They lookèd up and saw a star,
Shining in the east, beyond them far;
And to the earth it gave great light,
And so it continued both day and night:

And by the light of that same star,
Three Wise Men came from country far;
To seek for a king was their intent,
And to follow the star wheresoever it went:

This star drew nigh to the north-west;
O'er Bethlehem it took its rest,
And there it did both stop and stay
Right over the place where Jesus lay:

Then did they know assuredly
Within that house the King did lie:
One entered in then for to see,
And found the babe in poverty:

Then entered in those Wise Men three,
Fell reverently upon their knee,
And offered there in his presénce
Both gold and myrrh and frankincense:

Between an ox-stall and an ass
This child truly there born he was;
For want of clothing they did him lay
All in the manger, among the hay:

Then let us all with one accord
Sing praises to our heavenly Lord,
That hath made heaven and earth of naught,
And with his blood mankind hath bought:

If we in our time shall do well,
We shall be free from death and hell;
For God hath preparèd for us all
A resting place in general:
*Nowell, Nowell, Nowell, Nowell,*
*Born is the King of Israel!*

*Traditional*

# Snow Storm

What a night! The wind howls, hisses, and but stops
To howl more loud, while the snow volley keeps
Incessant batter at the window pane,
Making our comfort feel as sweet again;
And in the morning, when the tempest drops,
At every cottage door mountainous heaps
Of snow lie drifted, that all entrance stops
Until the beesom and the shovel gain
The path, and leave a wall on either side.
The shepherd rambling valleys white and wide
With new sensations his old memory fills,
When hedges left at night, no more descried,
Are turned to one white sweep of curving hills,
And trees turned bushes half their bodies hide.

The boy that goes to fodder with surprise
Walks oer the gate he opened yesternight.
The hedges all have vanished from his eyes;
Een some tree tops the sheep could reach to bite.
The novel scene emboldens new delight,
And, though with cautious steps his sports begin,
He bolder shuffles the huge hills of snow,
Till down he drops and plunges to the chin,
And struggles much and oft escape to win –
Then turns and laughs but dare not further go;
For deep the grass and bushes lie below,
Where little birds that soon at eve went in
With heads tucked in their wings now pine for day
And little feel boys oer their heads can stray.

*John Clare (1793–1864)*

# See, Amid the Winter's Snow

See, amid the winter's snow,
Born for us on earth below,
See, the tender lamb appears,
Promised from eternal years!

*Hail, the ever-blessed morn!*
*Hail, redemption's happy dawn!*
*Sing through all Jerusalem,*
*Christ is born in Bethlehem!*

Low within a manger lies
He who built the starry skies,
He who, throned in height sublime,
Sits amid the cherubim!

Say, ye holy shepherds, say:
What your joyful news today?
Wherefore have ye left your sheep
On the lonely mountain steep?

'As we watched at dead of night,
Lo! we saw a wondrous light;
Angels, singing 'Peace on earth',
Told us of the Saviour's birth.'

Sacred infant, all divine,
What a tender love was thine
Thus to come from highest bliss
Down to such a world as this!

Teach, oh teach us, holy Child,
By thy face so meek and mild,
Teach us to resemble thee
In thy sweet humility!

Virgin Mother, Mary blest,
By the joys that fill thy breast,
Pray for us that we may prove
Worthy of the Saviour's love.

*Edward Caswall (1814–1878)*

# A Winter Night

It was a chilly winter's night;
  And frost was glitt'ring on the ground,
And evening stars were twinkling bright;
  And from the gloomy plain around
  Came no sound,
But where, within the wood-girt tow'r,
The churchbell slowly struck the hour;

As if that all of human birth
  Had risen to the final day,
And soaring from the wornout earth
  Were called in hurry and dismay,
  Far away;
And I alone of all mankind
Were left in loneliness behind.

*William Barnes (1801–1886)*

# Winter

The boughs, the boughs are bare enough
But earth has never felt the snow.
Frost-furred our ivies are, and rough

With bills of rime the brambles shew.
The hoarse leaves crawl on hissing ground
Because the sighing wind is low.

But if the rain-blasts be unbound
And from dank feathers wring the drops
The clogged brook runs with choking sound

Kneading the mounded mire that stops
His channel under damming coats
Of foliage fallen in the copse.

A simple passage of weak notes
Is all the winter bird dare try
The bugle moon by daylight floats

So glassy white about the sky,
So like a berg of hyaline,
And pencilled blue so daintily,

I never saw her so divine
But through black branches, rarely drest
In scarves of silky shot and shine.

The webbèd and the watery west
Where yonder crimson fireball sits
Looks laid for feasting and for rest.

I see long reefs of violets
In beryl-covered fens so dim,
A gold-water Pactolus frets

Its brindled wharves and yellow brim,
The waxen colours weep and run
And slendering to his burning rim

Into the flat blue mist the sun
Drops out and all our day is done.

*Gerard Manley Hopkins (1844–1889)*

# Winter-Time

Late lies the wintry sun a-bed,
A frosty, fiery sleepy-head;
Blinks but an hour or two; and then,
A blood-red orange, sets again.

Before the stars have left the skies,
At morning in the dark I rise;
And shivering in my nakedness,
By the cold candle, bathe and dress.

Close by the jolly fire I sit
To warm my frozen bones a bit;
Or with a reindeer-sled, explore
The colder countries round the door.

When to go out, my nurse doth wrap
Me in my comforter and cap;
The cold wind burns my face, and blows
Its frosty pepper up my nose.

Black are my steps on silver sod;
Thick blows my frosty breath abroad;
And tree and house, and hill and lake,
Are frosted like a wedding cake.

*Robert Louis Stevenson (1850–1894)*

# Snow

In the gloom of whiteness,
In the great silence of snow,
A child was sighing
And bitterly saying: 'Oh,
They have killed a white bird up there on her nest,
The down is fluttering from her breast!'
And still it fell through the dusky brightness
On the child crying for the bird of the snow.

*Edward Thomas (1878–1917)*

# *from* As You Like It

Blow, blow, thou winter wind,
  Thou art not so unkind
    As man's ingratitude;
  Thy tooth is not so keen,
Because thou art not seen,
    Although thy breath be rude.
Heigh-ho! sing, heigh-ho! unto the green holly:
Most friendship is feigning, most loving mere folly:
  Then, heigh-ho, the holly!
    This life is most jolly.

  Freeze, freeze, thou bitter sky,
  That dost not bite so nigh
    As benefits forgot:
  Though thou the waters warp,
    Thy sting is not so sharp
    As friend remembered not.
Heigh-ho! sing, heigh-ho! unto the green holly ...
Most friendship is feigning, most loving mere folly:
  Then, heigh-ho, the holly!
    This life is most jolly.

*William Shakespeare (1564–1616)*

# Up in the Morning Early

Cauld blaws the wind frae east to west,
  The drift is driving sairly;
Sae loud and shrill's I hear the blast,
  I'm sure it's winter fairly.

CHORUS: Up in the morning's no for me,
  Up in the morning early;
When a' the hills are cover'd wi' snaw,
  I'm sure it's winter fairly.

The birds sit chittering in the thorn,
  A' day they fare but sparely;
And lang's the night frae e'en to morn,
  I'm sure it's winter fairly.

CHORUS: Up in the morning's no for me,
  Up in the morning early;
When a' the hills are cover'd wi' snaw,
  I'm sure it's winter fairly.

*Robert Burns (1759–1796)*

# In Tenebris

All within is warm,
  Here without it's very cold,
  Now the year is grown so old
And the dead leaves swarm.

In your heart is light,
  Here without it's very dark,
  When shall I hear the lark?
When see aright?

Oh, for a moment's space!
  Draw the clinging curtains wide
  Whilst I wait and yearn outside
Let the light fall on my face.

*Ford Madox Ford (1873–1939)*

# In the Bleak Midwinter

In the bleak midwinter
  Frosty wind made moan,
Earth stood hard as iron,
  Water like a stone;
Snow had fallen, snow on snow,
  Snow on snow,
In the bleak midwinter
  Long ago.

Our God, Heaven cannot hold Him,
  Nor earth sustain;
Heaven and earth shall flee away
  When He comes to reign.
In the bleak midwinter
  A stable place sufficed
The Lord God Almighty,
  Jesus Christ.

Enough for Him, whom cherubim
  Worship night and day,
A breastful of milk,
  And a mangerful of hay;
Enough for Him, whom angels
  Fall down before,
The ox and ass and camel
  Which adore.

Angels and archangels
  May have gathered there,
Cherubim and seraphim
  Thronged the air;

But His mother only,
   In her maiden bliss,
Worshipped the beloved
   With a kiss.

What can I give Him,
   Poor as I am?
If I were a shepherd,
   I would bring a lamb;
If I were a Wise Man,
   I would do my part;
Yet what I can I give Him:
   Give my heart.

               *Christina Rossetti*
               *(1830–1894)*

# It Came Upon the Midnight Clear

It came upon the midnight clear,
  That glorious song of old,
From angels bending near the earth
  To touch their harps of gold:
'Peace on the earth, good will to men,
  From heaven's all-gracious King!'
The world in solemn stillness lay
  To hear the angels sing.

Still through the cloven skies they come,
  With peaceful wings unfurled;
And still their heavenly music floats
  O'er all the weary world:
Above its sad and lowly plains
  They bend on hovering wing;
And ever o'er its Babel-sounds
  The blessed angels sing.

Yet with the woes of sin and strife
  The world has suffered long;
Beneath the angel-strain have rolled
  Two thousand years of wrong;
And man, at war with man, hears not
  The love-song which they bring:
O hush the noise, ye men of strife,
  And hear the angels sing.

For lo, the days are hastening on,
  By prophet-bards foretold,
When, with the ever-circling years,
  Comes round the age of gold;

When peace shall over all the earth
  Its ancient splendours fling,
And the whole world give back the song
  Which now the angels sing.

*Edmund Hamilton Sears*
*(1810–1876)*

# Snow in the Suburbs

Every branch big with it,
Bent every twig with it;
Every fork like a white web-foot;
Every street and pavement mute:
Some flakes have lost their way, and grope back
    upward when
Meeting those meandering down they turn and
    descend again.
The palings are glued together like a wall,
And there is no waft of wind with the fleecy fall.

A sparrow enters the tree,
Whereon immediately
A snow-lump thrice his own slight size
Descends on him and showers his head and eye
And overturns him,
And near inurns him,
And lights on a nether twig, when its brush
Starts off a volley of other lodging lumps with a rush.

The steps are a blanched slope,
Up which, with feeble hope,
A black cat comes, wide-eyed and thin;
And we take him in.

*Thomas Hardy (1840–1928)*

# *from* The Prelude

And in the frosty season, when the sun
Was set, and visible for many a mile
The cottage windows blazed through twilight gloom,
I heeded not their summons: happy time
It was indeed for all of us – for me
It was a time of rapture! Clear and loud
The village clock tolled six; I wheeled about,
Proud and exulting like an untired horse
That cares not for his home. All shod with steel,
We hissed along the polished ice in games
Confederate, imitative of the chase
And woodland pleasures – the resounding horn,
The pack loud chiming, and the hunted hare.
So through the darkness and the cold we flew,
And not a voice was idle; with the din
Smitten, the precipices rang aloud;
The leafless trees and every icy crag
Tinkled like iron; while far distant hills
Into the tumult sent an alien sound
Of melancholy not unnoticed, while the stars,
Eastward, were sparkling clear, and in the west
The orange sky of evening died away.
Not seldom from the uproar I retired
Into a silent bay, or sportively
Glanced sideway, leaving the tumultuous throng,
To cut across the reflex of a star
That fled, and, flying still before me, gleamed
Upon the glassy plain; and oftentimes,
When we had given our bodies to the wind,
And all the shadowy banks on either side
Came sweeping through the darkness, spinning still

The rapid line of motion, then at once
Have I, reclining back upon my heels,
Stopped short; yet still the solitary cliffs
Wheeled by me – even as if the earth had rolled
With visible motion her diurnal round!
Behind me did they stretch in solemn train,
Feebler and feebler, and I stood and watched
Till all was tranquil as a dreamless sleep.

*William Wordsworth (1770–1850)*

## *from* Frost at Midnight

The Frost performs its secret ministry,
Unhelped by any wind. The owlet's cry
Came loud – and hark, again! loud as before.
The inmates of my cottage, all at rest,
Have left me to that solitude, which suits
Abstruser musings: save that at my side
My cradled infant slumbers peacefully.
'Tis calm indeed! so calm, that it disturbs
And vexes meditation with its strange
And extreme silentness. Sea, hill, and wood,
This populous village! Sea, and hill, and wood,
With all the numberless goings-on of life,
Inaudible as dreams!

*Samuel Taylor Coleridge (1772–1834)*

# A Frosty Day

Grass afield wears silver thatch;
   Palings all are edged with rime;
Frost-flowers pattern round the latch;
   Cloud nor breeze dissolve the clime;

When the waves are solid floor,
   And the clods are iron-bound,
And the boughs are crystall'd hoar,
   And the red leaf nailed a-ground.

When the fieldfare's flight is slow,
   And a rosy vapour rim,
Now the sun is small and low,
   Belts along the region dim.

When the ice-crack flies and flaws,
   Shore to shore, with thunder shock,
Deeper than the evening daws,
   Clearer than the village clock.

When the rusty blackbird strips,
   Bunch by bunch, the coral thorn;
And the pale day-crescent dips,
   Now to heaven, a slender horn.

*Lord de Tabley (1835–1895)*

# Ice on the Highway

Seven buxom women abreast, and arm in arm,
  Trudge down the hill, tip-toed,
    And breathing warm;
They must perforce trudge thus, to keep upright
  On the glassy ice-bound road.

And they must get to market whether or no,
  Provisions running low
  With the nearing Saturday night,
While the lumbering van wherein they mostly ride
  Can nowise go:
Yet loud their laughter as they stagger and slide!

*Thomas Hardy (1840–1928)*

# Now Winter Nights Enlarge

Now winter nights enlarge
The number of their hours,
And clouds their storms discharge
Upon the airy towers.
Let now the chimneys blaze,
And cups o'erflow with wine;
Let well-tuned words amaze
With harmony divine.
Now yellow waxen lights
Shall wait on honey love,
While youthful revels, masques, and courtly sights
Sleep's leaden spells remove.

This time doth well dispense
With lovers' long discourse;
Much speech hath some defence,
Though beauty no remorse.
All do not all things well;
Some measures comely tread,
Some knotted riddles tell,
Some poems smoothly read.
The summer hath his joys
And winter his delights;
Though love and all his pleasures are but toys,
They shorten tedious nights.

*Thomas Campion (1567–1620)*

# NATIVITY

# Christmas

All after pleasures as I rid one day,
  My horse and I, both tir'd, bodie and minde,
  With full crie of affections, quite astray,
I took up in the next inne I could finde.
There when I came, whom found I but my deare,
  My dearest Lord, expecting till the grief
  Of pleasures brought me to him, readie there
To be all passengers most sweet relief?
O Thou, whose glorious, yet contracted light,
  Wrapt in nights mantle, stole into a manger;
  Since my dark soul and brutish is thy right,
To Man of all beasts be not thou a stranger:
  Furnish & deck my soul, that thou mayst have
  A better lodging then a rack or grave.


The shepherds sing; and shall I silent be?
              My God, no hymne for thee?
My soul's a shepherd too; a flock it feeds
              Of thoughts, and words, and deeds.
The pasture is thy word: the streams, thy grace
              Enriching all the place.
Shepherd and flock shall sing, and all my powers
              Out-sing the day-light houres.
Then we will chide the sunne for letting night
              Take up his place and right:
We sing one common Lord; wherefore he should
              Himself the candle hold.
I will go searching, till I find a sunne
              Shall stay, till we have done;
A willing shiner, that shall shine as gladly,
              As frost-nipt sunnes look sadly.

Then we will sing, and shine all our own day,
　　　　And one another pay:
His beams shall cheer my breast, and both so twine,
Till ev'n his beams sing, and my musick shine.

*George Herbert (1593-1633)*

# The Nativity

Peace? and to all the world? sure, one
And he the prince of peace, hath none.
He travels to be born, and then
Is born to travel more agen.
Poor Galilee! thou can'st not be
The place for his Nativity.
His restless mother's call'd away,
And not deliver'd till she pay.

  A Tax? 'tis so still! we can see
The Church thrive in her misery;
And like her head at Bethlem, rise
When she opprest with troubles, lyes.
Rise? should all fall, we cannot be
In more extremities than he.
Great Type of passions! come what will,
Thy grief exceeds all copies still.
Thou cam'st from heav'n to earth, that we
Might go from Earth to Heav'n with thee.
And though thou found'st no welcom here,
Thou did'st provide us mansions there.
A stable was thy Court, and when
Men turn'd to beasts, Beasts would be Men.
They were thy Courtiers, others none;
And their poor Manger was thy Throne.
No swadling silks thy Limbs did fold,
Though thou could'st turn thy Rays to gold.
No Rockers waited on thy birth,
No Cradles stirr'd: nor songs of mirth;
But her chast Lap and sacred Brest
Which lodg'd thee first, did give thee rest.

  But stay: what light is that doth stream,

And drop here in a gilded beam?
It is thy Star runs page, and brings
Thy tributary Eastern Kings.
Lord! grant some Light to us, that we
May with them find the way to thee.
Behold what mists eclipse the day:
How dark it is! shed down one Ray
To guide us out of this sad night,
And say once more, Let there be Light.

*Henry Vaughan (1622–1695)*

# Nativity

Immensity cloistered in thy dear womb,
Now leaves his well-beloved imprisonment,
There he hath made himself to his intent
Weak enough, now into our world to come;
But Oh, for thee, for him, hath th' Inn no room?
Yet lay him in this stall, and from the Orient,
Stars, and wisemen will travel to prevent
Th' effect of Herod's jealous general doom.
Seest thou, my Soul, with thy faith's eyes, how he
Which fills all place, yet none holds him, doth lie?
Was not his pity towards thee wondrous high,
That would have need to be pitied by thee?
Kiss him, and with him into Egypt go,
With his kind mother, who partakes thy woe.

*John Donne (c.1572–1631)*

# Upon Christ His Birth

Strange news! a city full? will none give way
To lodge a guest that comes not every day?
No inn, nor tavern void? yet I descry
One empty place alone, where we may lie:
In too much fullness is some want: but where?
Men's empty hearts: let's ask for lodging there.
But if they not admit us, then we'll say
Their hearts, as well as inns, are made of clay.

*Sir John Suckling (1609–1642)*

# Noel: Christmas Eve, 1913

*Pax hominibus benae voluntatis*

A frosty Christmas Eve
  when the stars were shining
Fared I forth alone
  where westward falls the hill,
And from many a village
  in the water'd valley
Distant music reach'd me
  peals of bells aringing:
The constellated sounds
  ran sprinkling on earth's floor
As the dark vault above
  with stars was spangled o'er.

Then sped my thought to keep
  that first Christmas of all
When the shepherds watching
  by their folds ere the dawn
Heard music in the fields
  and marveling could not tell
Whether it were angels
  or the bright stars singing.

Now blessed be the tow'rs
  that crown England so fair
That stand up strong in prayer
  unto God for our souls:
Blessed be their founders
  (said I) an' our country folk
Who are ringing for Christ
  in the belfries to-night

With arms lifted to clutch
   the rattling ropes that race
Into the dark above
   and the mad romping din.

But to me heard afar
   it was starry music
Angels' song, comforting
   as the comfort of Christ
When he spake tenderly
   to his sorrowful flock:
The old words came to me
   by the riches of time
Mellow'd and transfigured
   as I stood on the hill
Heark'ning in the aspect
   of th' eternal silence.

*Robert Bridges (1844–1930)*

## *from* In Memoriam

### CIV

The time draws near the birth of Christ;
   The moon is hid, the night is still;
   A single church below the hill
Is pealing, folded in the mist.

A single peal of bells below,
   That wakens at this hour of rest
   A single murmur in the breast,
That these are not the bells I know.

Like strangers' voices here they sound,
   In lands where not a memory strays,
   Nor landmark breathes of other days,
But all is new unhallowed ground.

### CV

Tonight ungathered let us leave
   This laurel, let this holly stand:
   We live within the stranger's land,
And strangely falls our Christmas-eve.

Our father's dust is left alone
   And silent under other snows:
   There in due time the woodbine blows,
The violet comes, but we are gone.

No more shall wayward grief abuse
   The genial hour with mask and mime;
   For change of place, like growth of time,
Has broke the bond of dying use.

Let cares that petty shadows cast,
   By which our lives are chiefly proved,
   A little spare the night I loved,
And hold it solemn to the past.

But let no footstep beat the floor,
   Nor bowl of wassail mantle warm;
   For who would keep an ancient form
Through which the spirit breathes no more?

Be neither song, nor game, nor feast;
   Nor harp be touched, nor flute be blown;
   No dance, no motion, save alone
What lightens in the lucid east.

Of rising worlds by yonder wood.
   Long sleeps the summer in the seed;
   Run out your measured arcs, and lead
The closing cycle rich in good.

*Alfred, Lord Tennyson (1809–1892)*

# Christmas Eve

Christmas hath a darkness
  Brighter than the blazing noon,
Christmas hath a chillness
  Warmer than the heat of June,
Christmas hath a beauty
  Lovelier than the world can show:
For Christmas bringeth Jesus,
  Brought for us so low.

Earth, strike up your music,
  Birds that sing and bells that ring;
Heaven hath answering music
  For all Angels soon to sing:
Earth, put on your whitest
  Bridal robe of spotless snow:
For Christmas bringeth Jesus,
  Brought for us so low.

*Christina Rossetti (1722–1771)*

# THE EARTHLY PARADISE

## *from* The Earthly Paradise

Outlanders, whence come ye last?
  *The snow in the street and the wind on the door,*
Through what green seas and great have ye passed?
  *Minstrels and maids stand forth on the floor.*

From far away, O masters mine,
We come to bear you goodly wine.

From far away we come to you,
To tell of great tidings strange and true.

News, news of the Trinity,
And Mary and Joseph from over the sea!

For as we wandered far and wide,
What hap do you deem there should us betide?

Under a bent when the night was deep,
There lay three shepherds tending their sheep:

'O ye shepherds, what have ye seen,
To slay your sorrow and heal your teen?'

'In an ox-stall this night we saw
A babe and a maid without a flaw:

'There was an old man there beside;
His hair was white and his hood was wide:

'And as we gazed this thing upon,
Those twain knelt down to the little one.

'And a marvellous song we straight did hear.
That slew our sorrow and healed our care.'

News of a fair and a marvellous thing,
Nowell, nowell, nowell, we sing.

*William Morris (1834–1896)*

# God Rest You Merry, Gentlemen

God rest you merry, gentlemen,
　　Let nothing you dismay,
Remember Christ our Saviour
　　Was born on Christmas Day,
To save poor souls from Satan's power
　　Which had long time gone astray,
And it's tidings of comfort and joy.

From God that is our Father,
　　The blessèd Angels came,
Unto some certain Shepherds,
　　With tidings of the same;
That there was born in Bethlehem,
　　The Son of God by name.
And it's tidings of comfort and joy.

Go, fear not, said God's Angels,
　　Let nothing you affright,
For there is born in Bethlehem,
　　Of a pure Virgin bright,
One able to advance you,
　　And threw down Satan quite.
And it's tidings of comfort and joy.

The Shepherds at those tidings,
　　Rejoiced much in mind,
And left their flocks a feeding
　　In tempest storms of wind,
And strait they came to Bethlehem,
　　The son of God to find.
And it's tidings of comfort and joy.

Now when they came to Bethlehem,
    Where our sweet Saviour lay,
They found him in a manger,
    Where Oxen feed on hay,
The blessed Virgin kneeling down,
    Unto the Lord did pray.
And it's tidings of comfort and joy.

With sudden joy and gladness,
    The Shepherds were beguil'd,
To see the Babe of Israel,
    Before his mother mild,
On them with joy and chearfulness,
    Rejoice each Mother's Child.
And it's tidings of comfort and joy.

Now to the Lord sing praises,
    All you within this place,
Like we true loving Brethren,
    Each other to embrace,
For the merry time of Christmas,
    Is drawing on a pace.
And it's tidings of comfort and joy.

God bless the ruler of this House,
    And send him long to reign,
And many a merry Christmas
    May live to see again.
Among your friends and kindred,
    That live both far and near
And God send you a happy New Year.

*Traditional*

# Carol

I sing the birth was born to-night,
The author both of life and light;
  The angels so did sound it,
And, like the ravished shepherds said,
Who saw the light, and were afraid,
  Yet searched, and true they found it.

The Son of God, the eternal king,
That did us all salvation bring,
  And freed our soul from danger,
He whom the whole world could not take,
The Word, which heaven and earth did make,
  Was now laid in a manger.

The Father's wisdom willed it so,
The Son's obedience knew no No;
  Both wills were in one stature,
And, as that wisdom had decreed,
The Word was now made flesh indeed,
  And took on him our nature.

What comfort by him we do win,
Who made himself the price of sin,
  To make us heirs of glory!
To see this babe, all innocence,
A martyr born in our defence,
  Can man forget the story?

*Ben Jonson (1572–1637)*

# Christmas at Sea

The sheets were frozen hard, and they cut the
    naked hand;
The decks were like a slide, where a seaman scarce
    could stand;
The wind was a nor'wester, blowing squally off
    the sea;
And cliffs and spouting breakers were the only
    things a-lee.

They heard the surf a-roaring before the break of day;
But 'twas only with the peep of light we saw how ill
    we lay.
We tumbled every hand on deck instanter, with a shout,
And we gave her the maintops'l, and stood by to go
    about.

All day we tacked and tacked between the South
    Head and the North;
All day we hauled the frozen sheets, and got no
    further forth;
All day as cold as charity, in bitter pain and dread,
For very life and nature we tacked from head to head.

We gave the South a wider berth, for there the
    tiderace roared;
But every tack we made we brought the North Head
    close aboard;
So's we saw the cliffs and houses, and the breakers
    running high,
And the coastguard in his garden, with his glass
    against his eye.

The frost was on the village roofs as white as
	ocean foam;
The good red fires were burning bright in every
	'longshore home;
The windows sparkled clear, and the chimneys
	volleyed out;
And I vow we sniffed the victuals as the vessel
	went about.

The bells upon the church were rung with a mighty
	jovial cheer;
For it's just that I should tell you how (of all days in
	the year)
This day of our adversity was blessèd Christmas
	morn,
And the house above the coastguard's was the house
	where I was born.

O well I saw the pleasant room, the pleasant faces
	there,
My mother's silver spectacles, my father's silver hair;
And well I saw the firelight, like a flight of homely
	elves,
Go dancing round the china-plates that stand upon
	the shelves.

And well I knew the talk they had, the talk that was
	of me,
Of the shadow on the household and the son that
	went to sea;
And O the wicked fool I seemed, in every kind of way,
To be here and hauling frozen ropes on blessèd
	Christmas Day.

They lit the high sea-light, and the dark began to fall.
'All hands to loose topgallant sails,' I heard the
captain call.
'By the Lord, she'll never stand it,' our first mate,
Jackson, cried.
... 'It's the one way or the other, Mr. Jackson,' he
replied.

She staggered to her bearings, but the sails were new
and good,
And the ship smelt up to windward just as though she
understood.
As the winter's day was ending, in the entry of the
night,
We cleared the weary headland, and passed below
the light.

And they heaved a mighty breath, every soul on board
but me,
As they saw her nose again pointing handsome out
to sea;
But all that I could think of, in the darkness and
the cold,
Was just that I was leaving home and my folks were
growing old.

*Robert Louis Stevenson (1850–1894)*

# Christmas in India

Dim dawn behind the tamarisks – the sky is saffron-
    yellow –
  As the women in the village grind the corn,
And the parrots seek the river-side, each calling to his
    fellow
  That the Day, the staring Eastern Day, is born.
    O the white dust on the highway! O the stenches
      in the byway!
      O the clammy fog that hovers over earth!
    And at Home they're making merry 'neath the
      white and scarlet berry –
      What part have India's exiles in their mirth?

Full day behind the tamarisks – the sky is blue and
    staring –
  As the cattle crawl afield beneath the yoke,
And they bear One o'er the field-path, who is past all
    hope or caring,
  To the ghat below the curling wreaths of smoke.
    Call on Rama, going slowly, as ye bear a brother
      lowly –
      Call on Rama – he may hear, perhaps, your
        voice!
    With our hymn-books and our psalters we appeal
      to other altars,
      And to-day we bid 'good Christian men rejoice!'

High noon behind the tamarisks – the sun is hot
    above us –
  As at Home the Christmas Day is breaking wan.
They will drink our healths at dinner – those who tell
    us how they love us,

And forget us till another year be gone!
O the toil that knows no breaking! O the
*heimweh*, ceaseless, aching!
O the black dividing Sea and alien Plain!
Youth was cheap – wherefore we sold it. Gold was
good – we hoped to hold it.
And to-day we know the fulness of our gain!

Grey dusk behind the tamarisks – the parrots fly
together –
As the Sun is sinking slowly over Home;
And his last ray seems to mock us shackled in a
lifelong tether
That drags us back howe'er so far we roam.
Hard her service, poor her payment – she is
ancient, tattered raiment –
India, she the grim Stepmother of our kind.
If a year of life be lent her, if her temple's shrine
we enter,
The door is shut – we may not look behind.

Black night behind the tamarisks – the owls begin
their chorus –
As the conches from the temple scream and bray.
With the fruitless years behind us and the hopeless
years before us,
Let us honour, O my brothers, Christmas Day!
Call a truce, then, to our labours – let us feast
with friends and neighbours,
And be merry as the custom of our caste;
For, if 'faint and forced the laughter,' and if
sadness follow after,
We are richer by one mocking Christmas past.

*Rudyard Kipling (1865–1936)*

# From East to West, From Shore to Shore

From east to west, from shore to shore,
  Let every heart awake and sing
The holy Child whom Mary bore,
  The Christ, the everlasting King.

Behold the world's Creator wears
  The form and fashion of a slave;
Our very flesh our Maker shares,
  His fallen creature, man, to save.

For this how wondrously he wrought!
  A maiden, in her lowly place,
Became, in ways beyond all thought,
  The chosen vessel of his grace.

She bowed her to the angel's word
  Declaring what the Father willed,
And suddenly the promised Lord
  That pure and hallowed temple filled.

He shrank not from the oxen's stall,
  He lay within the manger bed,
And he whose bounty feedeth all
  At Mary's breast himself was fed.

And while the angels in the sky
  Sang praise above the silent field,
To shepherds poor the Lord most high,
  The one great Shepherd, was revealed.

All glory for this blessed morn
    To God the Father very be;
All praise to thee, O Virgin-Born,
    All praise, O Holy Ghost, to thee.

*Traditional*

KINGS

# The Three Kings

Three Kings came riding from far away,
  Melchior and Gaspar and Baltasar;
Three Wise Men out of the East were they,
And they travelled by night and they slept by day,
  For their guide was a beautiful, wonderful star.

The star was so beautiful, large and clear,
  That all the other stars of the sky
Became a white mist in the atmosphere.
And by this they knew that the coming was near
  Of the Prince foretold in the prophecy.

Three caskets they bore on their saddle-bows,
  Three caskets of gold with golden keys;
Their robes were of crimson silk with rows
Of bells and pomegranates and furbelows,
  Their turbans like blossoming almond-trees.

And so the Three Kings rode into the West,
  Through the dusk of the night, over hill and dells,
And sometimes they nodded with beard on breast,
And sometimes talked, as they paused to rest,
  With the people they met at the wayside wells.

'Of the child that is born,' said Baltasar,
  'Good people, I pray you, tell us the news;
For we in the East have seen his star,
And have ridden fast, and have ridden far,
  To find and worship the King of the Jews.'

And the people answered, 'You ask in vain;
  We know of no king but Herod the Great!'
They thought the Wise Men were men insane,
As they spurred their horses across the plain,
  Like riders in haste, who cannot wait.

And when they came to Jerusalem,
  Herod the Great, who had heard this thing,
Sent for the Wise Men and questioned them;
And said, 'Go down unto Bethlehem,
  And bring me tidings of this new king.'

So they rode away; and the star stood still,
  The only one in the grey of morn;
Yes, it stopped, it stood still of its own free will,
Right over Bethlehem on the hill,
  The city of David where Christ was born.

And the Three Kings rode through the gate and
    the guard,
  Through the silent street, till their horses turned
And neighed as they entered the great inn-yard;
But the windows were closed, and the doors were
    barred,
  And only a light in the stable burned.

And cradled there in the scented hay,
  In the air made sweet by the breath of kine,
The little child in the manger lay,
The Child, that would be King one day
  Of a kingdom not human but divine.

His mother, Mary of Nazareth,
   Sat watching beside his place of rest,
Watching the even flow of his breath,
For the joy of life and the terror of death
   Were mingled together in her breast.

They laid their offerings at his feet:
   The gold was their tribute to a King,
The frankincense, with its odour sweet,
Was for the Priest, the Paraclete,
   The myrrh for the body's burying.

And the mother wondered and bowed her head,
   And sat as still as a statue of stone;
Her heart was troubled yet comforted,
Remembering what the Angel had said
   Of an endless reign and of David's throne.

Then the Kings rode out of the city gate,
   With a clatter of hoofs in proud array;
But they went not back to Herod the Great,
For they knew his malice and feared his hate,
   And returned to their homes by another way.

*Henry Wadsworth Longfellow (1807–1882)*

# We Three Kings

We three kings of Orient are;
Bearing gifts we traverse afar
Field and fountain, moor and mountain,
Following yonder star:

*O star of wonder, star of night,*
*Star with royal beauty bright,*
*Westward leading, still proceeding,*
*Guide us to thy perfect light.*

*Melchior.*
Born a king on Bethlehem plain,
Gold I bring, to crown him again –
King for ever, ceasing never,
Over us all to reign:

*Gaspar.*
Frankincense to offer have I;
Incense owns a Deity nigh:
Prayer and praising, all men raising,
Worship him, God most high:

*Balthazar.*
Myrrh is mine; its bitter perfume
Breathes a life of gathering gloom;
Sorrowing, sighing, bleeding, dying,
Sealed in the stone-cold tomb:

*All.*
Glorious now, behold him arise,
King, and God, and sacrifice!
Heaven sings alleluya,
Alleluya the earth replies:

> *O star of wonder, star of night,*
> *Star with royal beauty bright,*
> *Westward leading, still proceeding,*
> *Guide us to thy perfect light.*

*John Henry Hopkins (1820–1891)*

# As With Gladness Men of Old

As with gladness men of old
Did the guiding star behold,
As with joy they hailed its light,
Leading onward, beaming bright;
So, most gracious Lord, may we
Evermore be led to thee.

As with joyful steps they sped,
Saviour, to thy lowly bed,
There to bend the knee before
Thee whom heaven and earth adore;
So may we with willing feet
Ever seek thy mercy-seat.

As they offered gifts most rare
At thy cradle rude and bare,
So may we with holy joy,
Pure and free from sin's alloy,
All our costliest treasures bring,
Christ, to thee our heavenly King.

Holy Jesus, every day
Keep us in the narrow way,
And, when earthly things are past,
Bring our ransomed souls at last
Where they need no star to guide,
Where no clouds thy glory hide.

In the heavenly country bright
Need they no created light;
Thou its light, its joy, its crown,
Thou, its sun which goes not down;
There for ever may we sing
Alleluias to our King.

*William Chatterton Dix (1837–1898)*

# Good King Wenceslas

Good King Wenceslas looked out
  On the feast of Stephen,
When the snow lay round about,
  Deep and crisp and even;
Brightly shone the moon that night,
  Though the frost was cruel,
When a poor man came in sight,
  Gathering winter fuel.

'Hither, page, and stand by me,
  If thou knowst it, telling,
Yonder peasant, who is he?
  Where and what his dwelling?'
'Sire, he lives a good league hence,
  Underneath the mountain,
Right against the forest fence,
  By St Agnes' fountain.'

'Bring me flesh and bring me wine,
  Bring me pine logs hither,
Thou and I will see him dine,
  When we bear them thither.'
Page and monarch forth they went,
  Forth they went together,
Through the rude wind's wild lament
  And the bitter weather.

'Sire, the night is darker now
  And the wind grows stronger;
Fails my heart I know not how;
  I can go no longer.'

'Mark my footsteps, good my page;
  Tread thou in them boldly;
Thou shalt find the winter's rage
  Freeze thy blood less coldly.'

In his master's steps he trod
  Where the snow lay dinted;
Heat was in the very sod
  Which the saint had printed,
Therefore Christian men be sure,
  Wealth or rank possessing,
Ye who now will bless the poor.
  Shall yourselves find blessing.

*John Mason Neale (1818–1866)*

# The Mystic Magi

Three ancient men in Bethlehem's cave
  With awful wonder stand:
A voice had called them from their grave,
  In some far Eastern land.

They lived: they trod the former earth,
  When the old waters swelled,
The Ark, that womb of second birth,
  Their house and lineage held.

Pale Japhet bows the knee with gold,
  Bright Sem sweet incense brings,
And Cham the myrrh his fingers hold:
  Lo! the three orient Kings.

Types of the total earth, they hailed
  The signal's starry frame:
Shuddering with second life, they quailed
  At the Child Jesu's Name.

Then slow the Patriarchs turned and trod,
  And this their parting sigh:
'Our eyes have seen the living God,
  And now – once more to die.'

*Robert Stephen Hawker (1803–1875)*

# Kings Came Riding

Kings came riding
  One, two, and three,
Over the desert
  And over the sea.

One in a ship
  With a silver mast;
The fishermen wondered
  As he went past.

One on a horse
  With a saddle of gold;
The children came running
  To behold.

One came walking,
  Over the sand,
With a casket of treasure
  Held in his hand.

All the people
  Said, 'Where go they?'
But the kings went forward
  All through the day.

Night came on
  As those kings went by;
They shone like the gleaming
  Stars in the sky.

*Charles Williams (1886–1945)*

I SAW THREE SHIPS

# I Saw Three Ships Come Sailing In

I saw three ships come sailing in,
On Christmas Day, on Christmas Day,
I saw three ships come sailing in,
On Christmas Day in the morning.

And what was in those ships all three?
On Christmas Day, on Christmas Day,
And what was in those ships all three?
On Christmas Day in the morning.

Our Saviour Christ and his lady,
On Christmas Day, on Christmas Day,
Our Saviour Christ and his lady,
On Christmas Day in the morning.

Pray, whither sailed those ships all three?
On Christmas Day, on Christmas Day,
Pray, whither sailed those ships all three?
On Christmas Day in the morning.

O they sailed into Bethlehem,
On Christmas Day, on Christmas Day,
O they sailed into Bethlehem,
On Christmas Day in the morning.

And all the bells on earth shall ring,
On Christmas Day, on Christmas Day,
And all the bells on earth shall ring,
On Christmas Day in the morning.

And all the angels in heaven shall sing,
On Christmas Day, on Christmas Day,
And all the angels in heaven shall sing,
On Christmas Day in the morning.

And all the souls on earth shall sing,
On Christmas Day, on Christmas Day,
And all the souls on earth shall sing,
On Christmas Day in the morning.

Then let us all rejoice amain!
On Christmas Day, on Christmas Day,
Then let us all rejoice amain!
On Christmas Day in the morning.

*Traditional*

# As I Sat on a Sunny Bank

As I sat on a sunny bank
On Christmas day in the morning,
I saw three ships come sailing by
On Christmas day in the morning.
And who do you think were in those ships
But Joseph and his fair lady:
He did whistle and she did sing,
And all the bells on earth did ring
For joy our Saviour He was born
On Christmas day in the morning.

*Traditional*

# To-morrow Shall Be My Dancing Day

To-morrow shall be my dancing day:
   I would my true love did so chance
To see the legend of my play,
   To call my true love to my dance:

   *Sing O my love, O my love, my love, my love;*
   *This have I done for my true love.*

Then was I born of a virgin pure,
   Of her I took fleshly substance;
Thus was I knit to man's nature,
   To call my true love to my dance:

In a manger laid and wrapped I was,
   So very poor, this was my chance,
Betwixt an ox and a silly poor ass,
   To call my true love to my dance:

Then afterwards baptized I was;
   The Holy Ghost on me did glance,
My Father's voice heard from above,
   To call my true love to my dance:

   *Sing O my love, O my love, my love, my love;*
   *This have I done for my true love.*

*Traditional*

# The True Christmas

So stick up Ivie and the Bays,
And then restore the heathen ways.
Green will remind you of the spring,
Though this great day denies the thing.
And mortifies the Earth and all
But your wild Revels, and loose Hall.
Could you wear Flow'rs, and Roses strow
Blushing upon your breasts warm Snow,
That very dress your lightness will
Rebuke, and wither at the Ill.
The brightness of this day we owe
Not unto Music, Masque nor Showe:
Nor gallant furniture, nor Plate;
But to the Manger's mean Estate.
His life while here, as well as birth,
Was but a check to pomp and mirth;
And all man's greatness you may see
Condemn'd by his humility.

Then leave your open house and noise,
To welcom him with holy Joys,
And the poor Shepherd's watchfulness:
Whom light and hymns from Heav'n did bless.
What you abound with, cast abroad
To those that want, and ease your loade.
Who empties thus, will bring more in;
But riot is both loss and Sin.
Dress finely what comes not in sight,
And then you keep your Christmas right.

*Henry Vaughan (1622–1695)*

# A Visit from St Nicholas

'Twas the night before Christmas, when all through
   the house
Not a creature was stirring, not even a mouse;
The stockings were hung by the chimney with care,
In hopes that St Nicholas soon would be there;
The children were nestled all snug in their beds,
While visions of sugar-plums danced in their heads;
And mamma in her 'kerchief, and I in my cap,
Had just settled our brains for a long winter's nap –
When out on the lawn there arose such a clatter,
I sprang from my bed to see what was the matter.
Away to the window I flew like a flash,
Tore open the shutters, and threw up the sash.
The moon, on the breast of the new-fallen snow,
Gave the lustre of midday to objects below;
When, what to my wondering eyes should appear,
But a miniature sleigh and eight tiny reindeer,
With a little old driver, so lively and quick,
I knew in a moment it must be St Nick.
More rapid than eagles his coursers they came,
And he whistled, and shouted, and called them by
   name:
'Now, Dasher! now, Dancer! now, Prancer and Vixen!
On, Comet! on, Cupid! on, Donder and Blitzen!
To the top of the porch! to the top of the wall!
Now dash away! dash away! dash away all!'
As dry leaves that before the wild hurricane fly,
When they meet with an obstacle, mount to the sky;
So up to the house-top the coursers they flew
With the sleigh full of toys, and St Nicholas too.

And then, in a twinkling, I heard on the roof
The prancing and pawing of each little hoof –
As I drew in my head, and was turning around,
Down the chimney St Nicholas came with a bound.
He was dressed all in fur, from his head to his foot,
And his clothes were all tarnished with ashes and
     soot;
A bundle of toys he had flung on his back,
And he looked like a pedlar just opening his pack.
His eyes – how they twinkled; his dimples, how
     merry!
His cheeks were like roses, his nose like a cherry!
His droll little mouth was drawn up like a bow,
And the beard of his chin was as white as the snow;
The stump of a pipe he held tight in his teeth,
And the smoke it encircled his head like a wreath;
He had a broad face and a little round belly
That shook, when he laughed, like a bowl full of jelly.
He was chubby and plump, a right jolly old elf,
And I laughed when I saw him, in spite of myself;
A wink of his eye and a twist of his head
Soon gave me to know I had nothing to dread;
He spoke not a word, but went straight to his work,
And filled all the stockings; then turned with a jerk,
And laying his fingers aside of his nose,
And giving a nod, up the chimney he rose;
He sprang to his sleigh, to his team gave a whistle,
And away they all flew like the down of a thistle.
But I heard him exclaim, ere he drove out of sight,
'Happy Christmas to all, and to all a good night!'

*Clement Clarke Moore (1779–1863)*

# What Billy Wanted

Dear Santa Claus,
You brought a sledge
To me a year ago,
And when you come again, I hope,
You'll bring along some snow.

*Traditional*

# A Little Christmas Card

This little Christmas card has come,
  With greetings glad and gay,
To wish you all, both great and small,
  A merry Christmas Day.

Then when the festive day is past
  I'll just turn round, you see,
And wish you here a bright New Year,
  Quite full of mirth and glee.

And last your little Christmas card
  Will turn once more like this;
With smile so shy I'll say 'Good-bye,'
  And throw you each a kiss.

                    *Traditional*

# The Twelve Days of Christmas

On the first day of Christmas
My true love sent to me,
A partridge in a pear tree.

On the second day of Christmas
My true love sent to me,
Two turtle doves,
And a partridge in a pear tree.

On the third day of Christmas
My true love sent to me,
Three French hens, two turtle doves,
And a partridge in a pear tree.

On the fourth day of Christmas
My true love sent to me,
Four calling birds, three French hens,
Two turtle doves, and a partridge in a pear tree.

On the fifth day of Christmas
My true love sent to me,
Five gold rings, four calling birds,
Three French hens, two turtle doves,
And a partridge in a pear tree.

On the sixth day of Christmas
My true love sent to me,
Six geese a-laying, five gold rings,
Four calling birds, three French hens,
Two turtle doves, and a partridge in a pear tree.

On the seventh day of Christmas
My true love sent to me,
Seven swans a-swimming, six geese a-laying,
Five gold rings, four calling birds,
Three French hens, two turtle doves,
And a partridge in a pear tree.

On the eighth day of Christmas
My true love sent to me,
Eight maids a-milking, seven swans a-swimming,
Six geese a-laying, five gold rings,
Four calling birds, three French hens,
Two turtle doves, and a partridge in a pear tree.

On the ninth day of Christmas
My true love sent to me,
Nine drummers drumming, eight maids a-milking,
Seven swans a-swimming, six geese a-laying,
Five gold rings, four calling birds,
Three French hens, two turtle doves,
And a partridge in a pear tree.

On the tenth day of Christmas
My true love sent to me,
Ten pipers piping, nine drummers drumming,
Eight maids a-milking, seven swans a-swimming,
Six geese a-laying, five gold rings,
Four calling birds, three French hens,
Two turtle doves, and a partridge in a pear tree.

On the eleventh day of Christmas
My true love sent to me,
Eleven ladies dancing, ten pipers piping,
Nine drummers drumming, eight maids a-milking,

Seven swans a-swimming, six geese a-laying,
Five gold rings, four calling birds,
Three French hens, two turtle doves,
And a partridge in a pear tree.

On the twelfth day of Christmas
My true love sent to me,
Twelve lords a-leaping,
Eleven ladies dancing,
Ten pipers piping,
Nine drummers drumming,
Eight maids a-milking,
Seven swans a-swimming,
Six geese a-laying,
Five gold rings,
Four calling birds,
Three French hens,
Two turtle doves,
And a partridge in a pear tree.

*Traditional*

# NEW YEAR

# Another Christmas Gone

The first white hill still glistens
Beneath the moonlit skies;
As on the night of Christmas
Untrod it sleeping lies,
A new born year is waiting
To meet the early dawn:
And whisper this to all the world,
Another Christmas gone.

*Traditional*

# The Old Year

The Old Year's gone away
To nothingness and night:
We cannot find him all the day
Nor hear him in the night:
He left no footstep, mark or place
In either shade or sun:
The last year he'd a neighbour's face,
In this he's known by none.

All nothing everywhere:
Mists we on mornings see
Have more of substance when they're here
And more of form than he.
He was a friend by every fire.
In every cot and hall –
A guest to every heart's desire,
And now he's nought at all.

Old papers thrown away,
Old garments cast aside,
The talk of yesterday,
All things identified;
But times once torn away
No voices can recall:
The eve of New Year's Day
Left the Old Year lost to all.

*John Clare (1793–1864)*

# The New Year

Here we bring new water
From the well so clear,
For to worship God with,
This happy New Year.
Sing levy-dew, sing levy-dew,
The water and the wine;
The seven bright gold wires
And the bugles they do shine.
Sing reign of Fair Maid,
With gold upon her toe –
Open you the West Door,
And turn the Old Year go:
Sing reign of Fair Maid,
With gold upon her chin –
Open you the East Door,
And let the New Year in.

*Traditional*

# New Year

Word of endless adoration,
   Christ, I to thy call appear;
On my knees in meek prostration
   To begin a better year.

Spirits in eternal waiting,
   Special ministers of pray'r,
Which our welcome antedating,
   Shall the benediction bear.

Which, the type of vows completed,
   Shall the wreathed garland send,
While new blessings are intreated,
   And communicants attend.

Emblem of the hopes beginning,
   Who the budding rods shall bind,
Way from guiltless nature's winning,
   In good-will to human kind.

Ye that dwell with cherub-turtles
   Mated in that upmost light,
Or parade amongst the myrtles,
   On your steeds of speckl'd white.

Ye that sally from the portal
   Of yon everlasting bow'rs,
Sounding symphonies immortal,
   Years, and months, and days, and hours.

But nor myrtles, nor the breathing
   Of the never-dying grove,
Nor the chaplets sweetly wreathing,
   And by hands angelic wove;

Not the Musick or the mazes
   Of those spirits aptly tim'd,
Can avail like pray'r and praises
   By the Lamb himself sublim'd.

Take ye therefore what ye give him,
   Of his fulness grace for grace,
Strive to think him, speak him, live him,
   Till you find him face to face.

Sing like David, or like Hannah,
   As the spirit first began,
To the God of heights hosanna!
   Peace and charity to man.

Christ his blessing universal
   On th'arch-patriarch's seed bestow,
Which attend to my rehearsal
   Of melodious pray'r below.

       *Christopher Smart (1722–1771)*

# The New Year

I am the little New Year, ho, ho!
Here I come tripping it over the snow.
Shaking my bells with a merry din –
So open your doors and let me in!

Presents I bring for each and all –
Big folks, little folks, short and tall;
Each one from me a treasure may win –
So open your doors and let me in!

Some shall have silver and some shall have gold,
Some shall have new clothes and some shall have old;
Some shall have brass and some shall have tin –
So open your doors and let me in!

Some shall have water and some shall have milk,
Some shall have satin and some shall have silk!
But each from me a present may win –
So open your doors and let me in!

*Traditional*

# Auld Lang Syne

*For auld lang syne, my dear,*
*For auld lang syne.*
*We'll tak a cup o' kindness yet,*
*For auld lang syne.*

Should auld acquaintance be forgot
And never brought to mind?
Should auld acquaintance be forgot,
And auld lang syne?

And surely ye'll be your pint stoup,
And surely I'll be mine;
And we'll tak a cup o' kindness yet,
For auld lang syne.

We twa hae run about the braes,
And pou'd the gowans fine;
But we've wander'd mony a weary fit,
Sin' auld lang syne.

We twa hae paidl'd in the burn,
Frae morning sun till dine;
But seas between us braid hae roar'd
Sin' auld lang syne.

And there's a hand, my trusty fiere!
And gie's a hand o' thine!
And we'll tak a right gude-willie waught,
For auld lang syne.

*Robert Burns (1759–1796)*

# Ring Out, Wild Bells (*from* In Memoriam)

Ring out, wild bells, to the wild sky,
   The flying cloud, the frosty light:
   The year is dying in the night;
Ring out, wild bells, and let him die.

Ring out the old, ring in the new,
   Ring, happy bells, across the snow:
   The year is going, let him go;
Ring out the false, ring in the true.

Ring out the grief that saps the mind
   For those that here we see no more;
   Ring out the feud of rich and poor,
Ring in redress to all mankind.

Ring out a slowly dying cause,
   And ancient forms of party strife;
   Ring in the nobler modes of life,
With sweeter manners, purer laws.

Ring out the want, the care, the sin,
   The faithless coldness of the times;
   Ring out, ring out my mournful rhymes
But ring the fuller minstrel in.

Ring out false pride in place and blood,
   The civic slander and the spite;
   Ring in the love of truth and right,
Ring in the common love of good.

Ring out old shapes of foul disease;
  Ring out the narrowing lust of gold;
  Ring out the thousand wars of old,
Ring in the thousand years of peace.

Ring in the valiant man and free,
  The larger heart, the kindlier hand;
  Ring out the darkness of the land,
Ring in the Christ that is to be.

*Alfred, Lord Tennyson (1809–1892)*

# Farewell Old Year

Farewell old year,
With goodness crowned,
A hand divine hath set thy bound.

Welcome New Year,
Which shall bring
Fresh blessings
From Our Lord and King.

The old we leave without a tear,
The new we enter without fear.

*Traditional*

# New Every Morning

Every day is a fresh beginning,
Listen my soul to the glad refrain.
And, spite of old sorrows
And older sinning,
Troubles forecasted
And possible pain,
Take heart with the day and begin again.

*Susan Coolidge (1835–1905)*

# The Year

What can be said in New Year rhymes,
That's not been said a thousand times?

The new years come, the old years go,
We know we dream, we dream we know.

We rise up laughing with the light,
We lie down weeping with the night.

We hug the world until it stings,
We curse it then and sigh for wings.

We live, we love, we woo, we wed,
We wreathe our prides, we sheet our dead.

We laugh, we weep, we hope, we fear,
And that's the burden of a year.

*Ella Wheeler Wilcox (1850–1919)*

### *from* The Tempest

Our revels now are ended. These our actors,
As I foretold you, were all spirits and
Are melted into air, into thin air;
And, like the baseless fabric of this vision,
The cloud-capp'd towers, the gorgeous palaces,
The solemn temples, the great globe itself,
Yea, all which it inherit, shall dissolve
And, like this insubstantial pageant faded,
Leave not a rack behind. We are such stuff
As dreams are made on, and our little life
Is rounded with a sleep. Sir, I am vex'd;
Bear with my weakness; my old brain is troubled:
Be not disturb'd with my infirmity:
If you be pleased, retire into my cell
And there repose: a turn or two I'll walk,
To still my beating mind.

*William Shakespeare (1564–1616)*

# Index of Poets

Alexander, Cecil Frances   42

Baker, Theodore and Spaeth, Harriet R. K.   102
Baring-Gould, Sabine   41, 89
Barnes, William   129
Bingham, Clifton   10
Blake, William   85
Bridges, Robert   157
Brooks, Phillips   44
Burns, Robert   135, 213
Byrom, John   92

Campion, Thomas   147
Caswall, Edward   127
Chesterton, G. K.   40, 73, 84
Clare, John   18, 114, 126, 208
Cole, Charlotte Druitt   8
Coleridge, Mary Elizabeth   95
Coleridge, Samuel Taylor   144
Coolidge, Susan   217
Cullen, Countee   67

de Tabley, Lord   145
Dearmer, Percy   87
Dix, William Chatterton   184
Donne, John   155

Ford, Ford Madox   136

Hardy, Thomas   113, 119, 141, 146
Hawker, Robert Stephen   188
Herbert, George   151

Herrick, Robert   13, 71
Hopkins, Gerard Manley   130
Hopkins, John Henry   182

Jonson, Ben   169

Kipling, Rudyard   111, 173

Longfellow, Henry Wadsworth   179

Mohr, Joseph   66
Montgomery, James   49
Moore, Clement Clarke   198
Morris, William   23, 165

Neale, John Mason   186

Oakeley, F. and Brooke, W. T.   58

Paman, Clement   69

Reed, Edith M. G.   88
Rossetti, Christina   81, 82, 99, 100, 137, 161

Scott, Sir Walter   15
Sears, Edmund Hamilton   139
Shakespeare, William   134, 219
Smart, Christopher   75, 210
Southwell, Robert   77
Stevenson, Robert Louis   132, 170
Suckling, Sir John   156

Tate, Nahum   115
Tennyson, Alfred, Lord   159, 214

Thackeray, William Makepeace   103
Thomas, Edward   118, 133
Traditional   3, 4, 5, 6, 7, 9, 11, 26, 28, 30, 33, 34,
   37, 41, 46, 47, 52, 55, 56, 58, 64, 83, 88, 91, 94,
   101, 102, 105, 107, 116, 117, 120, 123, 124,
   167, 175, 193, 195, 196, 200, 201, 202, 207,
   209, 212, 216

Vaughan, Henry   63, 153, 197

Watts, Isaac   54
Wesley, Charles   50
Wilcox, Ella Wheeler   218
Williams, Charles   189
Woodward, George Ratcliffe   79
Wordsworth, William   14, 142

Yeats, W. B.   36

# Index of Titles

A Child this Day is Born  64
A Christmas Blessing  4
A Christmas Carol  84
A Cradle Song  85
A Dish for a Poet  11
A Frosty Day  145
A Hymn for Christmas Day  52
A Little Christmas Card  201
A Virgin Most Pure  34
A Visit from St Nicholas  198
A Winter Night  129
Advent  100
An Ode of the Birth of Our Saviour  71
Angels, from the Realms of Glory  49
Another Christmas Gone  207
As I Sat on a Sunny Bank  195
As With Gladness Men of Old  184
Auld Lang Syne  213
Away in a Manger  46

Before the Paling of the Stars  82
Birds at Winter Nightfall  119

Carol  169
Christmas  151
Christmas – A Song of Joy at Dawn  56
Christmas at Sea  170
Christmas Eve  161
Christmas in India  173
Christmas is Coming  3
Christmas Night  123

225

Christmas Plum Pudding  10
Christus Natus Est  67

December  18
Deck the Halls  6

Eddi's Service  111

Farewell Old Year  216
French Noel  23
*from* As You Like It  134
From East to West, From Shore to Shore  175
*from* Frost at Midnight  144
*from* In Memoriam  159
*from* The Earthly Paradise  165
*from* The Prelude  142
*from* The Tempest  219

Go, Tell it on the Mountain  116
God Rest You Merry, Gentlemen  167
Good King Wenceslas  186
Green Grow'th the Holly  101

Hark! The Herald Angels Sing  50
Here We Come A-Wassailing  28
Holly  99
Hymn for Christmas Day  92

I Saw a Stable  95
I Saw Three Ships Come Sailing In  193
I Sing of a Maiden  33
Ice on the Highway  146
In Dulci Jubilo  55
In Tenebris  136
In the Bleak Midwinter  137

Infant Holy   88
It Came Upon the Midnight Clear   139
It Was on Christmas Day   94

Joseph   40
Joy to the World!   54

Kings Came Riding   189

Little Robin Redbreast   120
Lo, How a Rose E'er Blooming   102
Love Came Down at Christmas   81

Minstrels   14

Nativity   155
New Every Morning   217
New Prince, New Pomp   77
New Year   210
Noel: Christmas Eve, 1913   157
Now Thrice Welcome, Christmas   5
Now Winter Nights Enlarge   147
Nowell Sing We   30

O Come, All Ye Faithful   58
O Little Town of Bethlehem   44
Old Christmastide   15
On Christmas Day to My Heart   69
Once in Royal David's City   42
Out in the Dark   118

Past Three O'Clock   79
Peace   63
Pudding Charms   8

Ring Out, Wild Bells (*from* In Memoriam)   214

See, Amid the Winter's Snow   127
Sheep in Winter   114
Silent Night   66
Sing Lullaby   89
Snow   133
Snow in the Suburbs   141
Snow Storm   126

The Angel Gabriel   41
The Cherry Tree Carol   37
The Christmas Pudding   9
The Coventry Carol   83
The First Nowell   124
The First Tree in the Greenwood   107
The Holly and the Ivy   105
The House of Christmas   73
The Mahogany Tree   103
The Mother of God   36
The Mystic Magi   188
The Nativity   153
The Nativity of Our Lord and
   Saviour Jesus Christ   75
The New Year   209
The New Year   212
The Old Hark   47
The Old Year   208
The Oxen   113
The Rocking Carol   87
The Shepherds' Carol   117
The Three Kings   179
The True Christmas   197
The Twelve Days of Christmas   202
The Year   218
To-morrow Shall Be My Dancing Day   196

Up in the Morning Early  135
Upon Christ His Birth  156

Wassail, Wassail  26
We Three Kings  182
We Wish You a Merry Christmas  7
Welcome to Heaven's King  91
What Billy Wanted  200
While Shepherds Watched Their Flocks  115
Winter  130
Winter-Time  132

Yule Log  13

## Index of First Lines

A child this day is born   64
A frosty Christmas Eve   157
A virgin most pure, as the prophets do tell   34
All after pleasures as I rid one day   151
All my heart this night rejoices   56
All within is warm   136
And in the frosty season, when the sun   142
Angels, from the realms of glory   49
Arise, and hail the sacred day!   52
Around the house the flakes fly faster   119
As I sat on a sunny bank   195
As with gladness men of old   184
Away in a manger, no crib for a bed   46

Before the paling of the stars   82
Behold, a silly tender Babe   77
Blow, blow, thou winter wind   134
But give me holly, bold and jolly   99

Cauld blaws the wind frae east to west   135
Christians awake, salute the happy morn   92
Christmas Eve, and twelve of the clock   113
Christmas hath a darkness   161
Christmas is coming   3
Christmas is here   103
Come, bring with a noise   13

Dear Santa Claus   200
Deck the halls with boughs of holly   6
Dim dawn behind the tamarisks – the sky is
   saffron-yellow   173

231

Earth grown old, yet still so green   100
Eddi, priest of St Wilfrid   111
Every branch big with it   141
Every day is a fresh beginning   217

Farewell old year   216
For auld lang syne, my dear   213
From east to west, from shore to shore   175

Glad Christmas comes, and every hearth   18
Go, tell it on the mountain   116
God bless the master of this house   4
God rest you merry, gentlemen   167
Good King Wenceslas looked out   186
Grass afield wears silver thatch   145
Green grow'th the holly   101

Hark! the herald angels sing   50
Hark, hark what news the angels bring   47
Heap on more wood! – the wind is chill   15
Here we bring new water   209
Here we come a-wassailing   28

I am the little New Year, ho, ho!   212
I saw a stable, low and very bare   95
I saw three ships come sailing in   193
I sing of a maiden   33
I sing the birth was born to-night   169
If the stars fell; night's nameless dreams   40
Immensity cloistered in thy dear womb   155
In Bethlehem   67
In dulci jubilo   55
In Numbers, and but these few   71
In the bleak midwinter   137
In the gloom of whiteness   133

Infant holy  88
Into the basin  9
It came upon the midnight clear  139
It was a chilly winter's night  129
It was on Christmas Day  94

Joseph was an old man  37
Joy to the world! the Lord is come  54

Kings came riding  189

Late lies the wintry sun a-bed  132
Little Jesus, sweetly sleep, do not stir  87
Little Robin Redbreast  120
Lo, how a Rose e'er blooming  102
Love came down at Christmas  81
Lully, lullay, thou little tiny child  83

Masters, in this Hall  23
My soul, there is a country  63

Now the holly bears a berry as white as the milk  107
Now thrice welcome, Christmas  5
Now winter nights enlarge  147
Nowell sing we, both all and some  30

O come, all ye faithful  58
O little town of Bethlehem  44
On the first day of Christmas  202
Once in Royal David's city  42
Our Christmas pudding was made in November  8
Our revels now are ended. These our actors  219
Out in the dark over the snow  118
Outlanders, whence come ye last?  165

Past three o'clock  79

Peace? and to all the world? sure, one  153

Ring out, wild bells, to the wild sky  214

See, amid the winter's snow  127
Seven buxom women abreast, and arm in arm  146
Silent night, holy night  66
Sing lullaby!  89
So stick up Ivie and the Bays  197
Softly, softly, through the darkness  123
Strange news! a city full? will none give way  156
Sweet dreams form a shade  85

Take a large olive, stone it and then stuff it with a
    paste made of anchovy, capers, and oil  11
The angel Gabriel from heaven came  41
The boughs, the boughs are bare enough  130
The Christ-child lay on Mary's lap  84
The first Nowell the angel did say  124
The first white hill still glistens  207
The Frost performs its secret ministry  144
The holly and the ivy  105
The minstrels played their Christmas tune  14
The Old Year's gone away  208
The sheep get up and make their many tracks  114
The sheets were frozen hard, and they cut the naked
    hand  170
The threefold terror of love; a fallen flare  36
The time draws near the birth of Christ  159
There fared a mother driven forth  73
This little Christmas card has come  201
Three ancient men in Bethlehem's cave  188
Three Kings came riding from far away  179
To Day  69

## Index of First Lines

To-morrow shall be my dancing day   196
'Twas the night before Christmas, when all through
  the house   198

Wassail, Wassail, all over the town!   26
We stood on the hills, Lady   117
We three kings of Orient are   182
We wish you a merry Christmas   7
Welcome to Thou, Heaven's King   91
What a night! The wind howls, hisses, and but
  stops   126
What can be said in New Year rhymes   218
When they sat down that day to dine   10
Where is this stupendous stranger?   75
While shepherds watched their flocks by night   115
Word of endless adoration   210

## MACMILLAN COLLECTOR'S LIBRARY

### Own the world's great works of literature in one beautiful collectible library

Designed and curated to appeal to book lovers everywhere, Macmillan Collector's Library editions are small enough to travel with you and striking enough to take pride of place on your bookshelf. These much-loved literary classics also make the perfect gift.

Beautifully produced with gilt edges, a ribbon marker, bespoke illustrated cover and real cloth binding, every Macmillan Collector's Library hardback adheres to the same high production values.

Discover something new or cherish your favourite stories with this elegant collection.

### Macmillan Collector's Library: own, collect, and treasure

*Discover the full range at*
macmillancollectorslibrary.com